PROPERTY of the REBEL LIBRARIAN

ALLISON VARNES

Random House 🏠 New York

Text copyright © 2018 by Allison Varnes
Jacket art copyright © 2018 by Andy Smith

All rights reserved. Published in the United States by
Random House Children's Books, a division of
Penguin Random House LLC, New York.

Random House and the colophon are registered trademarks of
Penguin Random House LLC.

Visit us on the Web! rhcbooks.com

Educators and librarians, for a variety of teaching tools,
visit us at RHTeachersLibrarians.com

Library of Congress Cataloging-in-Publication Data
Names: Varnes, Allison, author.
Title: Property of the rebel librarian / by Allison Varnes.
Description: First edition. | New York : Random House Books for Young
Readers, [2018] | Summary: Twelve-year-old June Harper, shocked when
her parents go on a campaign to clear the Dogwood Middle School library of
objectionable books, starts a secret banned books library in an empty locker.
Identifiers: LCCN 2018001349 | ISBN 978-1-5247-7147-8 (hardback) |
ISBN 978-1-5247-7149-2 (epub) | ISBN 978-1-5247-7148-5 (glb)
Subjects: | CYAC: Books and reading—Fiction. | Libraries—Fiction. |
Middle schools—Fiction. | Schools—Fiction. | Family life—Fiction. |
Protest movements—Fiction. | Librarians—Fiction. | BISAC: JUVENILE
FICTION / Books & Libraries. | JUVENILE FICTION / School & Education. |
JUVENILE FICTION / Social Issues / Adolescence.
Classification: LCC PZ7.1.V398 Pr 2018 | DDC [Fic]—dc23

Printed in the United States of America
10 9 8 7 6 5 4 3 2
First Edition

For Mom,
who read me stories,
and for Dad,
who told them

CONTENTS

RIPPLE EFFECTS

You're going to read a lot about me and the things I've done. Most of it's true.

I can't help that, not that I'd want to.

I would do the exact same thing all over again if I had the chance.

It's like when you read a sad book for the second time. You know *the moment* is coming, and you know it's going to make you cry, but that doesn't stop you. You read it anyway, because you love the story.

So take your time. I'll just be sitting here, grounded for all eternity, while you read about the moments when everything fell together and apart. They're all here. Every last one.

★

The front door swings open after I walk home from school, right on schedule. Except today, Dad holds my copy of *The Makings of a Witch*.

I grin up at him, but he doesn't return my smile.

The flush of rising blood pressure snakes across Dad's pale face to his ears. It looks like he raked his hand over his light brown hair a million times while pacing in front of the window. That's what he did when they finally let Kate go out on her first date. Back and forth, back and forth, right in front of the window until she showed up on the doorstep. Except she made curfew and then the show was over. This one is just getting started, and I have no idea why.

Dad signals to the empty spot by Mom on the love seat.

"Would you care to explain this?" he says, holding up the novel.

I shrug. "Um, it's a book?"

He stares at me through his tortoiseshell glasses until I look away. "Yes. One that we don't approve of."

I don't understand. They've always been okay with the books I've read. I squirm on the stiff cushions. "Dad, it's just a book. I—"

"What concerns me more than anything"—he taps the bar code sticker—"is that it's from the Dogwood Middle library, of all places."

The grandfather clock ticks away the seconds while I squirm. I can't watch TV or use the family computer without someone looking over my shoulder, but books have always been safe. Mom cross-stitched READERS ARE WINNERS on a couch pillow to prove it.

"Dad, I—"

"No buts, June. You know the rules."

Dad is president of the PTSA, and he keeps his thumb on everything at Dogwood Middle. Especially me. It doesn't matter that I'm twelve and have never, ever given Dad a real reason to worry. Did anyone ask me to the school dance last week? Nope. Why would they, when he'd follow us the whole time?

The best part of Dad's day is hassling my teachers about posting my grades online. Easy to do because he works from home as a tech consultant. It's so embarrassing. Sixth grade was bad enough, but things got ten times worse in August when Kate left for college.

Dad gently taps the novel against his knee. "Missing kids. Witches. It's too scary for you."

"No, it isn't! I *like* creepy stuff. If you'd just—"

3

"No. This sort of thing won't happen again. Understand, June, it's our job to protect you. It would be nice if you'd meet us halfway. Until you do, you're grounded. No TV. No phone. No internet."

"What?" I've never even been grounded before.

"You heard me. Rules are rules."

Mom shakes her head with disappointment.

Shame creeps up my face, making me flush red like I always do when I'm upset. I want to crawl under the couch. Was it wrong of me to read that book?

"I'll return it after school tomorrow," Mom says.

Oh no. Tomorrow is our last game of the season, and Mom will be there anyway because she runs the uniform closet for our marching band. I can't believe this is happening. Poor Ms. Bradshaw, the librarian, is going to get a visit from my mom, and then there won't be a hole big enough for me to hide in.

What have I done?

INTERCEPTED

I slip out the door with a breakfast bar in one hand and my house key in the other. Emma stands at the curb, squinting into the camera on her phone and putting on lip gloss her mom won't let her wear. It sparkles on her tan skin. Emma has her reasons for glamming it up, and they're all in the band. The middle school honors band started marching with the high school a few years ago. Their band was so small, they decided they needed seventh and eighth graders to look bigger. So this is the first year Emma and I get to take our instruments across the parking lot for sixth period, after-school practices, and football games. It's been two whole months since I started honors band, and I still get that little flutter in my stomach when I walk over to the high school. I wonder if that will ever go away.

I grin. "That's a great color on you." I swiped it for her from the stash Kate had abandoned under our bathroom sink when she left for college and stopped answering my calls.

Emma blots her lips and spritzes herself with Pretty as a Peach body spray. "Nice dress."

"Thanks. It has pockets," I say, holding out the sides of the green fabric as we start the long walk to school. It's maybe two miles to the middle school from here. Too close for the buses to pick up, and not far enough for my parents to drop their routines and drive me.

"What's the occasion?" Emma takes in my frizz-free hair and the necklace Kate gave me last Christmas and smiles a knowing smile. "You totally have a crush on Graham, don't you?"

My shoulders stiffen. "No." Like my parents would let me date an eighth grader. Or anyone.

"You like him!"

"Stop it."

"If you say so." Emma shrugs. "You're the one fainting everywhere."

"It was *one* time." I send her a sidelong glare. "I locked my knees, okay?" It was at band camp in July. My first-ever band camp, actually, since sixth graders aren't allowed to audition for honors band. We were standing in formation, and the next thing I knew, all I could see was blue sky and Graham's face. He caught me in the last moment before my head hit the pavement. Everyone flocked around me, but the truth is, he held me a moment too long. Past the moment of impact. Past the chorus of *Are you okay?* And then he winked and said, "Nice of you to drop in."

I groaned. "That's the worst joke I've ever heard."

He squinted at me. "Uh-oh. How hard did you hit your head?"

"I didn't hit my head."

He grinned. "It's the only explanation," he said as he pulled me to my feet. "Or trust me, you'd be laughing." Then he turned around and walked back to his spot like he was king of the universe. My mind turned to jelly, and I just stood there trying to think of a comeback.

You know how some people seem so unbelievably perfect, they can't possibly be real? Graham is like that. Always has been. It's like he's so sure of each step, and he's a total flirt. He's tall and blond, and his closet is full of designer plaid button-downs. Put him on a white horse, and he'd be galloping in the surf in a cologne ad. He probably knows it, too.

I could never be the girl on the horse. I once lost my balance on a carousel! So, no. I *don't* have a crush on Graham Whitmore. He's the boy I look at a second too long. Nothing more.

I change the subject and fill Emma in on everything with my parents, ending with, "And Mom'll be there later today to ruin my life. In a nutshell." I leave out the part about being grounded. It's too embarrassing.

Emma rolls her eyes. "It's just a book."

I laugh. "You know how they are." Emma has slept over enough times to know there's a 100 percent chance of G-rated movies before an early bedtime.

"My parents probably wouldn't care," she says.

I sigh and hop over the broken pieces of sidewalk where tree roots are pushing up through the concrete.

"Yeah," I say. "I know." Her parents aren't nearly as bad as mine are, but they don't have to be. Dad keeps constant tabs on both of us. Usually I don't mind that much. I don't really get in trouble. But being grounded for reading? That's a new one.

"Oh! Almost forgot." Emma digs *The Graveyard* out of her bag and hands it to me.

"You're done already?"

"Yeah. You'll love it. Read the beginning with the lights on, though."

I grin. "What's the matter, Em? Get a little scared?"

Emma rolls her eyes and gives my shoulder a playful shove. "You'll see what I mean."

"Okay, okay. I'll get it back to you soon."

Emma shrugs. "Just keep it."

"Seriously?" We share books all the time, but we always return them.

"It's yours. But you'll have to hide it from your parents because there are ghosts in it."

"Oh no, not *ghosts*! Thanks."

The houses end at the corner, and the sidewalk grows smooth again. We follow it across the street to the town square. It's the heart of everything, where parades and festivals are held every time a vegetable blooms. Flowers line the sidewalk in front of all the shops: pharmacy, post office, yoga studio, and everyone's favorite, the diner. Not that I get to spend much time there. From here, Dogwood Middle is less than a mile ahead.

"Think we'll win tonight?" Emma asks when the football field comes into view.

We haven't won a game since before Kate started high school. "Nope, but our band is better."

"Like there's any question."

With each step, my boots leave a trail of black scuff marks on the cement, as if to say *I was here*. It's oddly satisfying.

We stroll past Dogwood High, a two-story brick building built forty years ago, and up to its sister building, Dogwood Middle. Groups of kids hang out on the steps and the benches, laughing and talking.

The familiar smell of gym floors and sloppy joes hits my nostrils as we pass through the doors to the middle school. Several band members chat in the hallway, their instruments already in their hands. "See ya at the assembly?" Emma asks as we split up to go to our lockers.

"Sure." But I won't. I'm supposed to play fight songs to rally school spirit for the big game, but they'll need to have enough pep without me.

There's one place on my mind, and I should've been there ten minutes ago. But for the first time in my life, I'm nervous about going to the library. I'd give anything not to have to tell Ms. Bradshaw what's coming.

When I throw open the door, Ms. Bradshaw is stooped over an open box on a study carrel, her long auburn curls dangling over its contents.

The comforting smell of paper fills my lungs, and I relax a little. "Ms. Bradshaw?"

She plunks a stack of books on the table and glances up with a big grin on her rosy face. "Morning, June." Why does she have to look so happy to see me? She doesn't deserve what she's about to hear.

"Do you have a minute?"

She laughs. "Define *minute*. I've got to unload these before first period. Want to give me a hand and we can talk?"

"Yeah, okay." I flip through a few books I've never heard of: *Holes, Lily and Dunkin, Wishtree.*

"You'd like those," she says.

I put them down. My palms begin to sweat and my sad little breakfast gurgles in my stomach. *Tell her.* I take a deep breath and blurt out, "My parents found my copy of *The Makings of a Witch* and said I couldn't read it. My mom's bringing it back to you today. It's—it's bad."

Her eyes fall to the book in her hand, but she isn't really looking at it. She's probably thinking of how ridiculous my family is, because that's all I'm thinking about right now.

11

"I think they're mad it was in the library because of the witches and the graveyard. And the other stuff." There. Now she'll think twice before letting me rifle through the new titles.

She slaps a Dogwood Middle library sticker on the cover of the newest Percy Jackson book. "But you read it."

"I did."

"Then that's that," she says with a one-shouldered shrug. "There's nothing I can do about it."

"Tell that to my parents." I sigh. "They're probably going to make things difficult. I'm so sorry." I think I'm going to be sick. Ms. Bradshaw attends every single one of our football games, and she cheers the loudest during the halftime show.

"Did you like *The Makings of a Witch*?"

"I loved it. And here's the thing—it wasn't that scary. It kept me guessing what would happen next, but I didn't have nightmares or anything."

She reaches for her coffee mug on the other side of the box. "Is that right?"

"Yeah," I say quietly, and keep my eyes down, fiddling with the books on the table.

"You know, there's a reason I suggested it to you." She takes a slow sip of coffee and I can feel her staring at me.

"We wanted to work out the details before announcing it, but the author's coming next week to talk about her book. And you can't very well help run the event if you haven't read the book, can you?"

I look up at her and will myself not to let my jaw drop. "You're kidding me! She picked *Dogwood*?" We aren't exactly known for anything, really. There's an enormous pecan statue by the highway, but that's about it. It's also where cell phone service gets spotty. Try to get a bar of service to register here, and you could be waiting a long time.

Her expression settles into smooth, serious lines. "I don't kid about books. Ever." She nods toward a stack of flyers.

Now I know I'm in panic mode, or I never would've missed them. The book cover is in the center, with the event details listed below it. I can't believe it's actually happening. "This is so awesome."

She hands me a small stack. "Make yourself useful, would you? And of course you'll have to swing by afterward to say hello." She winks. "Can't let her leave without meeting library groupie number one."

"Seriously?"

She breaks into a huge smile. "It's already been

approved for fifth period next Thursday. School-wide assemblies are mandatory, last time I checked."

My heart sinks. There's no way it's going to happen for me. I'm not that lucky. "If you say so."

"Don't count yourself out just yet, June," she says, gathering a stack of books into her arms. "You read that one book, and one book can change everything."

★

By the end of fifth period, Ms. Bradshaw's flyers are all over the school. I've only hung one of mine. I had been hoping to wait until after my mom returned *The Makings of a Witch*. But the flyers pepper the library door, the drink machines, and even the math hallway. Ms. Bradshaw or other groupies have been hard at work. And if Mom sees them—and how could she possibly not?—it will just make things worse.

When I reach the high school band room next door, I'm about to jump out of my skin. I lace up my running shoes and drop my boots in a heap by the wall. Grabbing my case from the shelf, I put my flute together and sprint through the back door as fast as I can, my light brown ponytail swishing against my neck with every step.

"Come on!" Emma loops her skinny arm through mine and half walks, half drags me toward the field. "We're going to miss it!" I grin in spite of myself.

Emma loves being in high school band as much as I do. But I know there's a specific reason she's in a hurry now. Matt Brownlee. He's an eighth grader, and when he smiles, he shows off matching dimples. Emma and a few of the high school flute players won't stop talking about them.

Emma squeezes my arm. "Three o'clock." She nods toward Matt. He's chatting with the other baritones next to a gray car. My mother's car. I think I'm going to be sick. I guess Mom couldn't wait until after school.

"Emma," I say.

But her eyes are locked on Matt. "He's never had a girlfriend. How is that even possible?" Her short black hair is pulled back, the flyaway pieces secured with sparkly clips.

"Em," I say again, and grab her arm.

"What?"

I point to my mom's car. And of course Matt reaches for his Gatorade at that exact moment and sees my finger aimed in his direction. He raises an eyebrow. I turn away, cheeks burning brightly against my tan.

Emma's voice comes out as a hiss. "June! He saw you."

I shake my head and ignore her. I have bigger problems right now. "It's my mom's car," I hiss back at her.

Emma sucks in her breath. "Just try not to think about it—there's nothing you can do."

She's right. It's done, whatever it is. I dart a glance over my shoulder at the band room's back door, only to spot Brooke charging toward us. Mom is still nowhere in sight. "Wait up!" Brooke yells.

"Finally!" she gasps, trying to catch her breath. "Oh my gosh, so I'm in the hallway, and the old dude who teaches eighth-grade science stops me and asks where I'm going. I hold up my flute and I'm like, 'I'm late for band.' And then he tells me I can't be in the hall after the bell rings anymore unless I want a write-up." She rolls her eyes.

"Ugh, what's with that guy?" Emma says. "You were running to *honors* band! It's not like you were doing something really bad."

"Right?" Brooke exclaims, the freckles on her pale cheeks coming out in the sun.

"I've never even gotten a write-up. Have you?" Emma says.

"Nope." I glance back to Mom's car.

"Same. When are they going to realize they can trust us to do the right thing?" Brooke says.

I think about *The Makings of a Witch* and the "scary" scenes that made my parents so angry. "I don't know if they ever will," I say.

We trickle onto the path toward the stadium. After school, we practice on the student parking lot, but we can't do that when the cars are all still here. So we get to practice on the football field. I stare up at the stands in awe as we walk in—even without an audience, it feels exciting to play here.

"Hey, June," someone behind me says. Emma's eyes widen and she looks like she's about to say something. Graham. He falls into step with me and says, "I'm here if you need me to catch you."

I offer a smile that probably makes me look like I'm in pain, but that's generally what happens when I have to talk to cute guys. Strolling through the stadium gates and onto the track, I sneak a glance up at Graham. What am I supposed to say? *You're pretty*? Ugh. I kick a pebble into the grass.

I keep walking, trying not to look at him. Emma and Brooke tag along next to us, craning their necks to watch.

He shifts his trumpet to his other hand. "So, I was

17

wondering. You wanna go to the diner after the game? A bunch of us are going." He nods over at Emma and Brooke like they're an afterthought. "You guys can come, too."

Emma's face lights up like Christmas just came early. I'm tempted to turn around to make sure he's not talking to someone else. But he's staring at me, waiting for an answer. Is he asking me *out* out?

Like on a date? I wish I could tell him anything but the truth. It's so embarrassing. And I'm still really upset about it. "I don't think I'm allowed."

Emma whirls around. "She's allowed!"

"Emma!" This is hard enough without help.

His mouth twitches with amusement. "So, which is it?"

Emma looks like she's about to explode.

I know the diner will never happen. Even if I weren't grounded, there's still the whole no-dating rule. If it's even a date. But it's not like I can get in any *more* trouble today. "I'll ask."

"Great," Graham says.

The squeaks of the loudspeaker humming to life echo over the field. "It's heating up, guys, so let's do what we need to do and get back inside for fight tunes. We'll start at one in *two minutes*. Hurry up and get there."

The crowd disperses by section. Clarinets merge toward the flutes on the eastern side of the field, and trumpets, baritones, and tubas scurry to the opposite end.

"I'll catch you after the game," Graham says. Yep. And I'll catch the wrath of my parents. It'll be awesome.

The flute section awaits, and Emma and Brooke look like they're about to burst. But there's no time to talk. I'm not really feeling up to it anyway. Now I get to worry about telling Graham no *and* about Ms. Bradshaw. Graham is going to think I'm a princess locked in a tower who can't talk to boys, which is totally not true. My bedroom isn't in a tower.

We have just enough time to line up, and then the snare drum starts its cadence. Our band director, Mr. Ryman, decided to have a *Jaws* theme for our show this year. The best part is that we get to wear T-shirts that say WE'RE GONNA NEED A BIGGER BOAT. It's pretty much my idea of heaven. I can quote almost every line from the film (the edited, less scary version, of course).

We make it through the show twice. The third time, at the crescendo of the *Jaws* theme, the back door of the middle school bursts open like the building is on fire. Ms. Bradshaw follows, a box in her arms and her purse slung over her shoulder, and makes a beeline for her beat-up gold car. One of our school security guards steps out of the building behind her.

Something is majorly wrong.

This isn't a coincidence. My mom went to the library, and now Ms. Bradshaw is leaving. I want to sprint to the parking lot, but I'll be written up for sure if I go tearing off the field during class for no reason. All I can do is watch from a distance as Ms. Bradshaw slams her trunk shut. I know that everything happening to her is my fault. The *Jaws* theme makes it feel even more messed up.

I do my best not to get trampled by my section when her car peels out of the lot.

"Get it together, flutes!" Mr. Ryman says. "Act like you've done this before!"

But I'm hopeless. If I fall in line with any formation at all, it's by sheer habit and luck. I can't focus on anything other than finding out what happened to Ms. Bradshaw.

"Watch your step!" Emma yells over her shoulder in the show's final moments. "You almost ran right into me!"

We play the last note and snap our flutes into vertical positions in front of us. I march down the sideline and off the field to the beat of the snare. It doesn't feel like the afternoon before our last real game. It feels like a march to the gallows.

"Wake up, June!" Emma hisses. We exit in pairs through the main gate.

"Sorry," I mutter.

And I am. I'm so sorry I ever got caught.

EVERYBODY TALKS

I stake out the uniform closet the minute the final bell rings, but it's a total waste of time. Mom doesn't show until an hour before the game. It's not like her at all. She loves her role in the band.

"Mom," I say. "Did you see Ms. Bradshaw?"

"Not at first."

Not at first? "Okay, who did you see?"

"Principal Beeler. I showed him your book, and then we paid Ms. Bradshaw a visit."

Heat creeps into my face. "You could've just returned it," I say quietly.

She presses the iron to the maroon pants until the material yields in a perfect crease. Mom is good at getting everyone and everything to do what she wants. Even pants. "I could've, but what about other kids who might be exposed to it? It just wouldn't be right."

"And then?" I keep my voice calm. The better to cover the rush of panic I feel washing over me. What did she *do*?

Five clarinets pick that exact moment to check out their uniforms. She clears her throat, business as usual. "Now isn't the time, June. We'll discuss it later."

★

It's our last game of the year, and I'm sitting helpless in the stands gnawing on room-temperature pizza and listening to the gossip flying around me.

"I'm telling you," Brooke says from under sweaty bangs, "security doesn't run teachers off without reason." It sounds logical enough, except for one problem. There's no good reason to send Ms. Bradshaw away.

Emma smears ChapStick on her lips and gives me a small smile. She hasn't said a word since it happened.

"I bet she got accused of something, and now she's under investigation." Brooke removes her glasses and polishes them on her pants.

Emma glances at me, but she stays quiet, protecting my secret. I attack a hunk of crust much too large for me to chew. It's either that or tell Brooke about my mom, and then everyone will know that this is all my fault.

Something happened in that room to drive out Ms. Bradshaw. Something horrible enough to require a security escort. But what? Surely this can't be *all* Mom's doing? Or Dad's? I know they go overboard, but a scary book isn't enough to make them this mad . . . right?

The drum major climbs the podium and calls us to attention to play one of the twenty fight songs we have memorized. But I can't focus. I'm not in the mood to cheer for anything. I crack open a Coke, even though I know I can't play my flute for the next hour unless I want the sugary syrup to collect on the key pads like sap. I guzzle the drink.

Using the back of my white glove as a napkin, I survey the track. From dozens of yards away, my parents seem normal. They lean over the fence in their band booster shirts and jeans, looking like they actually care about organized sports. Even from way up here, I can still make out the outline of a great white shark on the backs of their shirts.

Mr. Beeler, the principal, is in intense conversation with them—probably over how to ruin my life. He looks

24

over his shoulder and scans my row until his eyes locate me, seated with Coke in hand while everyone around me plays on cue.

Before I can move an inch, Mom turns and zeroes in on my quiet rebellion. I jump to my feet and fling down the can.

But it's too late. The damage is done. She shakes her head. I can hear it now. *"June, you really wanted that flute, didn't you?"* and *"I'm so glad we invested in something you could destroy without a moment's thought."*

My shoulders drop. I wish I could stop disappointing my parents. And now I can kiss any chance of going to the diner goodbye.

★

When the game ended, Mom was still fuming. She would've whisked me away from everyone as quickly as possible, especially after I had the nerve to ask if I could go for burgers to celebrate the last game of the season. But she had to run the uniform closet, so all she could say was "Absolutely not!" right in front of Emma and Brooke. No surprise there. At least she didn't broadcast that I was grounded.

I lean back in my chair and wait. Brooke slicks her

hair back into a fresh ponytail and dusts powder on her cheeks. Emma coughs inside a cloud of her sweet peach body spray. I don't know why they're getting ready. The diner's not happening, and now I have to tell an eighth grader—*that* eighth grader—that I'm not coming. Why didn't I just say no when he asked?

I'm still stewing over how unfair my life is right now when a duffel bag drops to the floor on my right. Graham grins down at me. "I'm starving," he says. "Who's up for some onion rings?"

My stomach gets that flippy feeling as soon as I hear his voice. This is going to be so painful.

"Sure, I'll go," Emma says, zipping her bag shut.

My jaw would hit the floor if it weren't attached to my face.

"Count me in," Brooke says.

Wait. What? How can they do this when they know I can't go?

"How about it, June? Are you allowed?" Graham asks.

It takes everything in me to find my voice. "No," I say. "Not tonight."

His face actually falls like he's disappointed. "Oh, okay."

Maybe it *was* a date? And now I'll never know for sure.

"Maybe next time," I say. This is the last game. There's no next time unless it's an after-school thing.

"Sure. Next time." He nods at the door. "My mom said she'd give us a ride." His mom drives a fancy blue SUV.

I try not to look wounded. But I am. And then he's out the door with Brooke without a second glance.

"Hey." Emma hangs back for a moment. "Is this okay?"

I pretend like I'm looking for something in my bag. "Why wouldn't it be?"

"I just—you don't even like him. I didn't think you'd care."

I shrug. "I don't care." She knows I'm lying, but she leaves anyway.

The whole ride home is miserable. I'm caught between being in deep trouble, wanting to ask twenty questions about Ms. Bradshaw, and thinking about what it would be like to sit at a booth with Graham.

"Do you want to pay for a complete repadding?" Mom asks.

"No, ma'am." I want to tell her that I didn't play my flute at all, so the Coke couldn't have hurt it, but I'd probably just get into more trouble.

"I didn't think so. Maybe you should start thinking

about babysitting next summer. I refuse to pay for something you purposely did."

Dad speaks up. "That's if she doesn't go to a summer enrichment program." He looks over his shoulder at me. "You're going to apply soon."

That means no band camp. I'm not sure this day could get worse.

We pull into the driveway, and I trudge into my weekend prison. Dad's keys clatter across the side table, and he disappears into his office to answer emails. In the kitchen, the ice maker whirs and plinks cubes against Mom's glass. This isn't the time, but I won't be able to sleep tonight if I don't know. I have to know.

Mom flops down on the couch and places her glass on a coaster.

"Hey, Mom?"

She drops her head and rubs gentle, counterclockwise circles into her temples with her thumbs. "What?" Her shoulder-length brown hair falls around her face like a helmet.

"Where did Ms. Bradshaw go?"

She sighs. "Who says she went anywhere?"

"Mom, I saw a security guard walk her out of the

school, and so did a hundred band kids. Secret's out. Why did they make her leave?"

She parts her curtain of hair to look at me and presses her lips together. "It turns out there are things we didn't know about Ms. Bradshaw."

I wait. Ms. Bradshaw doesn't seem like the type to have deep, dark secrets. Mom says nothing.

"Well, are you going to tell me?"

"Not tonight." She takes a slow sip of iced tea.

How would Kate handle this? She's always so good at getting what she wants. When my parents first enacted their no-party policy, she didn't let that stop her. Kate insisted that she'd be attending an "academic celebration" at her friend's house. And it *worked*. No, Kate would never come right out and say it. But I'm not Kate, and I'm already grounded.

"I don't get why Ms. Bradshaw was forced to leave. I read a book, you returned it. People read books all the time."

"Not those books."

Stay calm. "Mom, I've read worse."

"Have you, now?" The ice clinks against her glass.

I square my shoulders and raise my chin. "Yes." I don't feel half as brave as I sound.

She kicks off her shoes and props up her feet on the ottoman. "It's time you went to bed."

Dismissed. Swatted away like a pesky mosquito buzzing around her ear.

I haul my bags up to my room. I drop everything when I see the bookshelf in the corner. It's empty.

Every. Single. Book.

Gone.

I charge down the stairs to the living room to find Mom curled up with my dog-eared copy of *The Hobbit*. Next to her, Dad reads *The Little Prince*.

I look from one to the other. "What did you do with my books?"

Mom turns a page and keeps reading.

"They're in safekeeping until we can make sure they're quality reading material." Dad takes off his reading glasses and massages the bridge of his nose.

"What?" I don't understand them at all.

"You will request books through us. If we have read a book and approve, we will release it to you," Dad says calmly.

"You can't be serious."

"We are. This is how it's going to be from now on."

"I think we should have a family discussion about it," I say.

"We've already had one. Now, if I'm not mistaken, I believe you're grounded."

I walk as heavily as I dare back to the stairs without actually stomping, and sneak a glance over my shoulder. They look so cozy snuggled up with my books. I don't get it. My books have nothing on the bathroom stalls at school, and I don't see my parents demanding a paint job. How is this happening? I always follow the rules! I can't believe I'm actually in trouble!

What would Kate say about all this? The few times I've called her, I've left messages like "It's ME. Your sister. Why don't you love me anymore?" and "I am pleased to inform you that you've won a cruise. Please reply with your credit card number, and you will enjoy nine glorious nights in the Caribbean." No return call yet.

Tonight is different, though. She's the only person on the planet who could possibly understand how I feel. I swipe my parents' phone from their nightstand and dial the number I've committed to memory. One ring. Two rings.

"Hello?"

I could cry. Finally. "Kate! It's me."

"June! Hey! I was going to call you back. I've just had a lot going on here."

I ignore her excuse and jump right in. "Mom and Dad have lost it, Kate. Like, they're being *ridiculous,* and I don't know what to do."

She laughs. "What else is new?"

My throat tightens. "They took my books."

"Wait—your *books*? Why?"

"I don't know. They think they're too scary? Because they could? I just—"

"June? Who are you talking to?" My mom's sharp tone cuts across the line. No, no, no. I finally manage to get Kate on the phone, and I can't tell her anything.

"Hi, Mom," Kate says.

"Honey!" Mom says. "Oh, it's so good to hear your voice!" At least we agree on that. Two months was too long. "June, you're grounded. Hang up the phone now."

"But Mom!"

"Now," she says.

Kate says, "Wait! Love you, June. We'll talk later."

"Love you, too," I croak. I click off the phone and drop it onto the bed. I tiptoe to the top of the stairs and catch a few snippets from Mom's end of the conversation like "inappropriate choices" and "totally unlike her."

I creep down a few steps and sit hugging my knees. Did I really make an inappropriate choice? I don't think so. But my parents have never been this mad. I wish I could hear Kate's side of the conversation. This doesn't make sense. Nothing makes sense.

"Love you, too, honey," Mom says, and hangs up the phone. Her voice echoes up the stairwell. "That went well."

"Yep. Hello, teenage years," Dad says.

Mom says something muffled, and then, "I just don't get why June would even want to read books like that."

"Same reason she and Emma snuck and watched that horror movie last summer."

They both laugh.

"She slept with the hallway light on for a week," Mom says.

I did *not*. I forgot to turn it off.

"But it's not just that book that bothers me; it's the others, too. And she's had them for how long? I never dreamed we'd need to monitor *kids' books*."

"I know," Dad says.

"What are we going to do with her?"

There's a brief silence. "Stay firm. She's testing us," Dad says.

"She can test all she wants. This is how it's going to

be." Mom groans. "The look on her face, though. Our child hates us."

"Our house, our rules. She'll get over it."

I lean my head against the wall.

Dad chuckles. "We sound like our parents."

"We do, don't we?" She sighs. "Good. They would've done the same thing."

I slink back into my room and stumble over my bag. I know I'm the one who left it on the floor, but it still feels like getting kicked by the universe. The perfect ending to a perfect day. I sling the bag against the wall and close my eyes.

And then I realize they didn't take *every* book. They couldn't, because one wasn't there. I dig *The Graveyard Book* out of my bag. Good thing they missed it. They'd freak out for sure at the beginning.

By the time Dad opens my door to check on me, the book is safely stashed under my nightstand, my light is out, and I'm grinning under the covers.

CONSEQUENCES

Mom has an early yoga class in town today before her volunteer group meeting, so she insists on giving me a ride to school. She can pretend she's just being nice, but the real reason is so I can't hang out with Emma. It's long-term planning for my punishment. Fine by me. I don't know if I even want to see Emma after Friday.

"Have a good day," Mom says.

I give her a tight-lipped grimace and tumble out of the passenger side of the car.

I walk down the hallway, not paying attention to anyone around me. I'm not thinking of anything at all, really, and yet I find myself in front of the library.

A sign on the door reads CLOSED FOR INVENTORY.

I try the handle anyway. Locked.

And then someone's hands cover my eyes and it all goes dark.

"Guess who?"

"Graham?" I whirl around and almost stumble over my own feet.

He takes one look at me and says, "Hey, you all right?"

It's weird, but for the first time, I'm not nervous talking to him. "Not really. I'm grounded forever."

"I heard," he says. "And I'm sorry. We missed you on Friday night." He shifts his weight to the other foot.

"Wait. You heard what?" I'll bet Emma found out I was grounded and blabbed it. Or maybe it was Graham's mom. Word travels fast around here.

He glances down the hallway and lowers his voice. "Look, I'm not supposed to be telling you this, but . . . I heard about your book, June. And I know what happened to Ms. Bradshaw."

I look back at the door at the mention of her name. The flyers are gone. I almost can't bring myself to ask, but I have to know. "Where is she?"

"My mom said she's been put on leave," Graham says.

"For what? Having *The Makings of a Witch* in the library? I don't understand."

"They didn't like it, but that wasn't the only reason."

"What? What else could she have done?" My stomach drops. I was so sure Ms. Bradshaw couldn't have done anything really bad. But Graham's mom is in the PTSA with my dad. Whatever he knows, it's probably true. I hold my breath and wait for him to answer.

"It was the author talk. Mr. Beeler had no idea what the book was about, and there he was on the program in black and white. It was embarrassing. They're all ticked at Ms. Bradshaw for not giving them more details."

I shake my head. "So she's in trouble because the principal didn't read the book?"

"I guess so," Graham says.

I sigh. "At least that's all." But in my heart I know there's more. "They canceled everything, didn't they?"

He fumbles with a thread on his button-down. "I'm really sorry, June. But yeah, the author isn't coming."

I lean my head against the wall.

He reaches for my hand. I don't twitch or pull away from him, even though I'm pretty sure my sweaty hand feels like a cold, wet fish.

"My parents took my books this weekend. *All* of them."

"I'm so sorry. That's awful." He squeezes my hand and my stomach does that flippy thing again. "Everyone will forget about it in a week." His voice is so reassuring, like it's the simplest solution in the world.

"I won't."

"No. I guess not."

"The whole thing is so unfair. I just checked out a book. And now Ms. Bradshaw is fired?"

"Not fired. Just on leave. It's like she's grounded, I guess." He studies me with his ice-blue eyes. "I'm really sorry *you're* grounded." He sighs. "You've completely ruined my plans, June. I was supposed to be cool and smooth and ask you out, and you were supposed to say yes. Just so you know."

I stifle a laugh. "That was cool and smooth? You dropped the ball on that one." I hold my shoulders a little straighter. I finally had a good comeback!

He winks. "You haven't seen anything yet."

★

When I get to art class, Emma is already sitting at our regular table swirling her brush in the water jar and sending an inky cloud of royal blue spiraling out to the sides. I sit down next to her.

"So, how was Friday?" I ask. Part of me doesn't even want to know, but I have to ask.

She pauses midstroke with her brush and flashes her best smile. "It was awesome! Tons of people were there. Oh, and Matt even showed up with his dad." She flushes the tiniest bit. "Wish you could've come."

"Sounds like you had a blast without me."

"Aw, come on, June. It's never as fun when you're not there."

I shrug.

"All Graham wanted to talk about was you, anyway. It was all, 'What does June like? What's her favorite flower?' and stuff like that." She singsongs, "I think someone likes you!"

It's all I can do not to break into a huge grin.

Emma starts to say something else, then stops. Her eyes follow my pencil sketch. "I missed you this morning. When were you going to tell me you're grounded?"

I erase a smudge and blow the eraser fragments off my paper. "Looks like I didn't need to."

"Would've been nice to know."

"My mom snapped at me about the diner right in front of you. What more did you want?"

"It's not the same thing."

"But you still went to the diner without me." I can't even look at her when I say it.

Emma paints in silence for a moment. "I told him you hate daisies. They look like white-and-yellow weeds." She waves her hand at the flowers in front of her. This is Emma's best attempt at an apology in years. Then again, it's not like we ever fight.

I nod and go along with it. "And they smell like a funeral parlor." They're arranged in a rusty watering can meant to be adorable and quaint.

"You think all flowers smell like a funeral parlor."

I finish my pencil sketch of the last maple leaves clinging to a tree branch. "True."

"Have you been to a lot of funerals or something?"

"No. That's just what they smell like," I insist.

"You're so weird."

I shrug. I may be weird, but Graham Whitmore likes me. I smile thinking about him finding me at the library this morning. Like he knew I might need a friend.

I pick up a short, rounded brush and set to work

blending water and the tiniest dot of red pigment into a small pool.

Emma leans closer to the watering can and examines a petal. "Well, if Matt sent me a dozen roses, I'd put them out where everyone could smell them. Even you."

"Can't wait."

"So what's Graham supposed to get you when you go out? Assuming your parents ever let you leave the house again."

"He doesn't have to get me anything."

"No, no. I mean, what would make you happy?" Emma presses.

I touch the tip of my brush to the canvas and lay the base of watercolor. "Something that lasts. Flowers die."

Mr. Garcia strolls up to us and leans over my painting, resting his chin on his hand like he's trying to solve a complex problem. He taps his fingers against his brown skin and short brown beard. "What's your vision for this, June? All watercolor?"

I tilt my head to study it. "I'm not really sure yet. I'm just seeing where it goes."

He nods. "You don't have to go any heavier. Each layer of watercolor will take it a shade deeper. The challenge," he says, "is not doing too much too soon. Let it dry, then repeat. Slow and steady. That's the way to do it."

He moves over to Emma's painting. "I see you like the opaque, Ms. Davenport."

"Huh?"

"You like strong, solid color."

"Oh yeah," she says. "Blue's my favorite."

"I can see that," he says, walking to the next table.

Emma rolls her eyes. "I hate art."

★

I make it to the band room with a few minutes to spare before the sixth-period bell rings. This door has a sign on it, too, except it reads NO AFTER-SCHOOL PRACTICE DUE TO WEATHER. That's weird. Even if it's storming, we still have indoor rehearsal. We'll keep practicing the halftime show for the next few weeks in the hope we'll be invited to play in another competition. After that, we'll start rehearsing for the Christmas parade.

Everyone's already set up in sections with music stands and everything. I dump my stuff next to Brooke and hurry to the instrument room to dig out my flute.

Mr. Ryman rings the dinner bell, also called the triangle, which is his way of calling us to order when we're inside. I hustle out and slip into my chair, flute at the ready.

"As you've all seen, after-school practice is canceled, so we've got to focus extra hard during class today."

I whisper to Brooke, "What's going on?"

"There's some kind of meeting in the auditorium. All the teachers have to go."

"For what?"

"Don't know. Something big. People in suits were standing in front of the office during class change. A bunch of people from the PTSA will be there, too."

This just keeps getting worse. I've never really gotten in trouble in my life and now the PTSA is involved? My nose starts to tingle and I know I'm going to start to cry if I don't pull myself together. I take a deep breath and start playing warm-up scales on my flute.

We play the *Jaws* show twice—just long enough for Mr. Ryman to start making corrections to each individual song.

My mind races through the events of the last few days. Graham knew something, but I bet Mom knows more. Maybe I can get her to tell me what it's all about when I get home. I just need to ask the right questions. As for Dad, he's probably already here.

When the final bell rings, the room clears out. Most people are running for the buses, but I take my time putting away my flute. It's raining and the walk home won't be fun.

"Ready?" Emma says by the door.

I pull up my hood, and we run through the sideways rain into the parking lot. I don't know why we even bother with raincoats. We're going to get drenched anyway. Days like this shouldn't exist for kids who have to walk home.

Emma points through the downpour. "Hey, isn't that your mom's car?"

She's right. There's a PROUD PARENT OF A DOGWOOD HONOR STUDENT sticker on the back. I'm not sure Mom's so proud of me right now. And the sticker is for Kate anyway.

If Mom is here, I'm staying here. Then maybe I can get her to answer my questions on the drive home. "Yeah, I'm going to hang out in the band room and catch a ride with her."

"She's probably at that meeting. You'll be here forever," Emma says.

I look at the sky and shrug. "Beats this."

She nods. "K. I'm going home. I've got to get going on my research paper."

44

I run back to the band room. In the back corner, Matt Brownlee strums his guitar. His eyes follow me as I settle into a chair. The melody of an old song fills the room while I shiver, soaking wet, in the air conditioning.

Matt stops playing. "Rough day?" His eyebrows are raised in expectation, but I'm not saying much. I don't even know him.

"Something like that. Why are you still here?" I toss my wet raincoat onto an empty chair.

"I'm waiting for my dad to get off work. You?"

"My mom has a meeting," I mumble. He looks more at home with a guitar than a baritone, I decide as I rummage through my backpack for a hair tie.

Matt's fingers drift across the strings. "No book?"

I didn't think he even knew who I was, and he notices when I'm missing my usual prop? "No," I say. There's no telling what he's heard about Ms. Bradshaw, and I'm not adding fuel to the fire.

He plays the first chord. "You sing?"

"Only when no one's listening."

He grins, his smile bright against his band practice tan. "I could be no one."

My cheeks flame. Emma would die if she could see this. I don't know what to say. "I, um, I . . ."

He grins and belts out the first line of the song. I pull out my math book and stare at it instead of his dimples, but the singing doesn't stop. After a while, I hum a little bit. Before I know it, I'm singing along. I know all the words because I've heard it a million times on the radio in my parents' cars.

Matt looks proud.

"So, why this song?" I ask.

"Why not?"

"It's not something most kids listen to."

He shrugs. "Because—I don't know. I can't explain it." He stops strumming. "Why do you read the books you read?"

I think for a moment. Entertainment, sure, but what makes a book entertaining? I like a good tearjerker as much as I love a comedy. And the way I barricade the door when I'm reading something scary is kind of why I'm currently grounded. I think. "Because they make me feel more than I would if I were just living. I feel things when I read." Jeez, I sound so weird.

His expression softens. "That's why this song."

That deserves an encore. "Fine," I say. "Play the chord." And I sing. It's not great, but it's not bad, either. I love Matt's voice. He sounds like a cross between a rocker and a pop star, gravelly but still able to hit the high notes. We're singing the chorus again when Mom walks into the room and drops her jaw.

She takes in his raggedy jeans and his tanned bare feet balanced on the rungs of his chair. "June! What are you still doing here?"

"I saw your car," I say. "I thought I'd just wait for you." And ask you a million questions on the way home that you probably won't answer, but I can dream.

"You should've just gone home. I can't believe you've been here this whole time!" She sneaks another look at Matt, as though she also can't believe I've been alone with him.

"Where's Dad?"

"He's still finishing up." There's a long, awkward pause. "Hmm. I guess we should go," she says. "I would wait it out if I thought the rain might stop soon." What she means is that she would wait out the storm if she didn't need to separate me from Matt. Please. Like he'd ever be interested in me. "Grab your stuff, June." She hovers in the doorway. "Hurry. It's coming down even harder now."

Matt strums the guitar again. "Nah," he says. "It's just a little shower."

Mom and I walk as quickly as we can through the downpour to the car. It's only when I'm inside with my seat belt buckled that I realize I'm still humming.

★

The next day at lunch, the line in the cafeteria is moving extra slowly. I think I know why. "What do you mean, you don't serve bacon bits anymore?"

The lunch lady's eyebrows shoot up in exasperation under her hairnet. "New health guidelines. No bacon."

I look down at my brownish lettuce leaves and a few watery pieces of bruised tomato. "Okay," I say, trying a new strategy. "What do you serve?"

She points to two tubs on ice. "Fat-free ranch or vinaigrette. Take your pick."

I ladle a white glop onto my salad. "May I have a roll?"

"No."

I look up at her. "Really?"

She nods toward a basket of whole-wheat crackers.

I swipe a pack, enter my code at the register, and plop down at my usual table next to Emma. I'm frowning at my tray when Graham says, "Everything tastes better with ketchup." He slides into the seat next to me and offers me a ketchup packet. I'd pinch myself to see if I'm dreaming, but I don't want to know.

Say something smart, something funny, something—"Rabbit food doesn't." Fail.

He shrugs. "You were expecting burgers?"

"No . . . but if they're trying to make us healthy, brown lettuce isn't going to do it. We're going to starve!"

Brooke takes the seat next to Graham and dumps a peanut butter and jelly sandwich and a cookie double-stuffed with cream out of her brown bag.

"Trade you," I offer. "One lovely salad with dressing in exchange for the sandwich and the cookie. It doesn't get any better than that. You know you want it." I wiggle my eyebrows at Brooke.

She laughs. "I'll pass."

"Have you guys heard anything about the library?" I ask. Maybe if I could get in there, I could find some way to contact Ms. Bradshaw. Like an email address or something. I could start apologizing now, but I still wouldn't be done by Christmas. And to top it all off, I couldn't get my mom to say a word about the meeting yesterday.

Graham shakes his head. "The inventory sign is still on the door."

"I kind of like the library being closed," Emma says.

My head snaps toward her in disbelief. I open my mouth and then she says, "You're usually running off in the middle of lunch, but now I get to spend the whole period with you!"

"I guess that's a silver lining," I say. But I still miss spending the last ten minutes of lunch getting new book recommendations from Ms. Bradshaw. I shove a stale whole-wheat cracker in my mouth, and my stomach rumbles in protest. This can't last forever. I'm so packing my lunch tonight.

Graham smiles at me. "Maybe *I* should eat with you guys more often."

A sharp kick connects with my shin under the table. "Ow!" I glance at Emma, who calmly stabs her juice pouch with a straw. The corners of her mouth twitch like they do when she's trying not to laugh.

"What?" Graham asks.

I shoot a dirty look at Emma. "Nothing." I glance at Graham. "What would happen if we all packed our lunches? Just think about it—no more cafeteria food." I poke a straw into my milk carton and ball up the wrapper.

Brooke says, "I wouldn't feel bad eating cookies in front of you anymore."

I throw the wrapper at her. "No, seriously. What would they do?"

"Cry? They can't make us buy it," Emma says.

"Do you think the food would get better?"

"Not a chance," Brooke says. "Most of us already bring our lunches because the food is so bad."

"But not everyone does. If we did, they would lose money and then . . ."

Graham frowns at my salad. "They can't fix *that*."

I scowl at the brown leaves. "Yeah, you're probably right," I say. But if I could, I'd fix everything that's wrong with this school.

One thing at a time.

EXTRACTION

I step out of the shower to a ringing phone. "Mom! Can you get that?" The phone rings again. I wrap myself in a towel and sprint down the hall just in time to swipe the phone from my parents' nightstand. "Hello?"

"Hey," Emma says. She never calls this early because we have to use the landline. My parents say I'm not old enough for a cell phone, so I'm probably the only seventh grader without one. It feels like it, anyway.

"Hey. What's up?"

"I just wanted to let you know my mom's taking me to school today. We'd take you, too, but we're leaving now."

"Why so early?"

She yawns. "I wish I knew, but she's in a big hurry."

Her voice drops to a whisper. "I think it might have some-thing to do with the—" Emma's mom cuts her off, yelling about getting in the car.

"About what?" I ask.

"Sorry, I have to go. I'll see you at school." The phone clicks off before Emma even says goodbye.

I flip through my closet quickly so I can get to school and figure out what that was all about. I grab a pair of skinny cords and a lacy white T-shirt. I add a long navy cardigan. I tug on flat brown boots and scurry into my bathroom to dry my hair. I say it's *my* bathroom, but Kate's stuff is still everywhere for when she comes home on school breaks. If she comes home. I snuck a call last night and left yet another message for her, but I'm not getting my hopes up. I'm totally on my own now. I place a small dab of lip gloss in the center of my bottom lip and then press my lips together.

Downstairs, a note from my parents awaits on the kitchen counter:

Left early for errands. Have a good day! Love, Mom and Dad.

That's weird. Maybe my parents' presence at the meeting this week has something to do with it. But what could possibly be so important that they had to leave before dawn? Nothing is open this early. And they never leave without saying bye. Ever.

I toast an English muffin and smear it with peanut butter. Then I load up the biggest tumbler I can find with hot chocolate, because Mom isn't here to prevent my sugar rush. I also take a moment to pack my lunch so I won't have to eat cafeteria mystery meat.

The rain moved out overnight, leaving behind blue skies and lots of puddles. There's a reason we still have mosquitoes in October in the South. Still, the air is new, with a crisp bite to it, and I breathe it in with each careful, measured step over the cracked sidewalk. If my family wants to complain about something, it should be this. This uneven cement could actually hurt someone.

The stop sign looms ahead, right where it always is. Except this time, I don't go where I always go. I turn left.

Maple Lane is older than my street, with giant trees lining the curb. The houses have been around since my parents were kids. There is no sidewalk here. But there's also no traffic.

I love this street, but this is the long way to school. I thought I wanted to get to school early, but the more

I think about what might be waiting for me—or not waiting for me—the more I want to take my time.

Maple is out of the way. It's quiet. It's just the change I need today. When I was little, I'd fly down the street on my bike, tassels streaming, leaves crunching under my tires. The memory floods me with warmth, and for the first time since last week, I feel like I'm exactly where I'm supposed to be.

About midway down the street, a small house with pink flowers still in bloom brings me to a halt. Balanced on a tall wooden post, right by the curb, is some sort of dollhouse. I've never seen anything like it. I lean in closer. Below its top two windows, a glass door protects a few books on the other side. LITTLE FREE LIBRARY is engraved in a metal plate at the top, with the inscription TAKE A BOOK, LEAVE A BOOK just below it.

I feel like I just found a wad of cash, but better. I still have plenty of time, and the street is just as empty as it was before. Inside the box, there are a few magazines and *The Secret Horses of Briar Hill*.

I pull the novel off the shelf and pause. I don't have one to leave at the moment. But I have a whole library being held hostage at home. I can always make it an even trade later. I flip my bag around and slip the book into the main compartment.

I don't even notice the rest of the walk to school. I'm too busy thinking about when I'm going to curl up with my newest novel.

When I get to the middle school, two moving trucks are parked in the pickup/drop-off circle. They're probably full of athletic equipment for our football team. Meanwhile, the marching band has worn the same uniforms since my parents were students here.

Emma isn't at her locker, so I wander off to the library to check the status. The CLOSED FOR INVENTORY sign is still up, and the door is locked. I'm about to turn away when the door creaks open, revealing a heaping cartload of books behind it. I hold the door while two older men wheel the cart into the hallway. Then I slip inside.

The space is almost unrecognizable. Rolling carts line the walls, and volunteers transfer stacks of books onto them. Huge gaps linger on the shelves where large quantities of books used to be. Just like my bedroom bookshelf, but grander in scale.

Front and center, of course, are my parents.

"Dad!" He freezes with a novel in his hand. "What are you doing?" He tosses the book into the half-full bin.

"We're reviewing the inventory."

I take in the full carts next to them. "It looks like you're getting *rid* of the inventory."

"It's called a book extraction." He plucks another novel off the shelf and flings it into the offending pile.

"What? Why?" I'm not even sure what to ask.

"It's necessary for quality control."

My eyes tear up, to my total horror. But I won't let them see me cry. I blink back the tears as best I can. "Dad." My voice comes out in a whisper because it would crack if I tried to speak more loudly.

I turn my head all the way to the left so I don't have to look at him, and I wish I hadn't. There's Emma, standing by her own cart brimming with books. And next to her, Graham. "You? You're in on this?" So much for my voice not cracking. I don't even know which one I'm talking to. I try to form more words, but they won't come. My heart does a little flippy movement in my chest. Emma *lied* to me. Or at least she didn't try very hard to tell me what was going on. But why? And Graham held my hand, and I thought he—

"June, I—" Emma takes a step toward me, but I spin on my heel and let the door slam shut behind me. What do I care if I'm locked out now?

By the time I get to science, I feel like my head is going to explode. Since when does this school get so worked up about *books*?

And Emma! My molars grind together. She knows how much I love the library, but it didn't matter. *I* didn't matter. But why? And with Graham? It just doesn't make sense.

Ms. Langford distributes a stack of papers right as the bell rings. "I'm handing out a new resolution passed by our school board. Please make sure to take it home to your parents. Initial the form I'm sending around to show you received it."

Olivia hands it back to me over her straight blond hair. I take one and pass the stack to the next person.

Dear Parents, Students, Teachers, and Community Members:

Several resolutions were passed during a board meeting this week to address recent events. Please read the changes carefully, as they directly impact all of us in the Dogwood community. It follows that:

No reading beyond the textbook may be assigned unless the teacher has completed and posted the Reading Clarity Form to his or her web page. Teachers will indicate whether a book contains the following: profanity, drugs, violence, rock/rap music, witchcraft, drinking, smoking, or rebellion of any kind. Administration and parents must approve the text prior to classroom coverage, or instruction will be limited to the designated textbook.

Effective immediately, Dogwood school libraries will no longer house texts that contain any of the aforementioned components. They are hereby banned for unsupervised distribution.

Students in possession of unapproved texts will face disciplinary action. Teachers in violation of this resolution will be terminated.

The paper shakes in my hand. I read the last two sentences again, trying to make sense of them. I was wrong before. *Now* I'm going to be sick. Just like that, I can't read a book at home or in the library.

Ms. Langford clears her throat, her lipstick bright against her pale skin. "The office has asked me to note that if you're caught with a banned book, there will be consequences. Don't be that person they'll make an example of for the entire school."

For the first time I can remember in recent years, most of my classmates are silent. Everybody is shocked.

I mean, who thought books would be cause for punishment? Well, everybody except one.

Madison Greene laughs and shakes her brown curls over her shoulders. "Why would we even care what they keep in the library? It's not like we're busting down the door to get in there." She would've cared back when we were still friends. But that was a long time ago.

Ryan says, "Because they think we shouldn't be able to choose what we read, that's why."

"So what?" Madison says. "Who actually reads?" She looks at me with piercing blue eyes, her expression emotionless.

I stare back.

"That's enough," Ms. Langford says. "We're not going to talk about it in this classroom. It's not up for debate."

She must be taking lessons from my mom.

★

I wait my turn at the sink in art class to fill my water cup.

"I didn't want to do it," Emma says. "My parents made me."

I flip the knob on the faucet too hard and spray water all over myself. "They *made* you?"

Emma hands me a paper towel. "Yeah. Just like yours

made you hand over *The Makings of a Witch*. It was like 'Get in the car, or else' this morning. My mom didn't give me a choice."

I mop up the mess and swipe a palette from the counter.

"June, come on." Emma nudges my shoulder playfully. "I tried to tell you, but my mom freaked when she heard me whispering!" She chooses a few shades of blue paint. "I wanted to tell you the moment I found out about it. The whole thing was so unfair. And then you saw me and thought I was *with* them."

"I can't get that image out of my mind."

"Tell me about it," Emma says. "I actually tried to slip a book into my bag for you, but my dad caught me."

I look up at her then and smile before I can stop myself. "I just wish you'd told them no." I shake my head and squeeze red paint onto my palette. "I wouldn't have done any of it. Not even if they grounded me until Christmas."

Emma selects a midlength brush. "You don't really know what you'd do until you're the one with the choice."

★

I've never skipped a class in my life. I don't steal. I follow the rules. I've never even been sent to the principal's office.

I've never had a reason until now.

When the lunch bell rings, I tell Brooke I'm going to the bathroom. I'm not going there now, but I will later, so it's not a lie. Not technically. When I'm far enough away, I slip outside and follow the path to the deserted outdoor patio. I think it used to be a popular lunch spot, but the tables are old and a lot of the chairs are broken so no one eats here anymore. But I don't care about broken chairs. I only care about one thing right now and it's in my backpack. It may be against the rules, but I need to tune everything else out and read. With my jacket rolled into a pillow, I curl up on the bench and open *The Secret Horses of Briar Hill*. There's a message written in elegant loops of blue ink:

To Brendan,
I'll always see the real you.

It's so personal, I feel like I'm not supposed to be reading it. But it *was* in the Little Free Library, so I guess it's okay. I speed through the opening pages and eat my turkey sandwich. I'm already wondering why no one else can see the horses, when I'm shaken out of my thoughts by the sound of my name.

Mr. Hawkins towers over me with a cup of coffee. Of all the teachers to catch me, he's the worst. He's always scowling, and he looks like he's about to have a heart attack most of the time. Then again, if I were the detention teacher, I'd freak out, too.

"June," he says again. "What are you reading?"

There are a million things I could do right now. I could run. I could lie. I could make excuses. But I do none of these things. I hold up the book and wait for his response.

"I see. And who approved it?"

"No one."

He sighs. "Then I have to write it up. I've also got to confiscate the book."

I hand it over, panic blooming in my heart. A write-up? Me? I can't believe this is happening. I knew reading was against the rules, but that's why I came out here to do it.

And now I'll never know if the horse comes back.

I don't bother going to the cafeteria after that. I'm not really in the mood to see Emma and definitely not Graham, so I just wait in the classroom for Honors English to start. I tap my pencil against my desk. What will my parents say when they find out what I've done? I feel sick to my stomach. Midway through examples of hyper-bole, the classroom phone rings.

"Yes?" Ms. Gibson says. She listens for a moment. "I'll send her right up." She places the phone on the receiver and looks at me funny, her black skin creasing with concern around her eyes. "June, Mr. Beeler needs to see you."

My stomach drops and my heart starts racing. My first trip to the principal's office. Ever. Everyone stares while I gather my things with shaking hands.

The ladies in the front office frown as I slip past their desks, and so does Mr. Beeler. "Please sit down," he says. I settle into the stained fabric chair in front of Mr. Beeler's desk. He takes a long sip out of his coffee mug. There's a cartoon fish on the front of it that says GET HOOKED. His eyes bore holes into me, so I stare at the walls and try not to squirm. A rainbow trout hangs in a frame behind him. Next to it there's a photo of Mr. Beeler, his face and hair gleaming white in the sun, holding a fishnet by a shore-line. Clearly, he likes catching things.

I don't belong here.

"Now, Ms. Harper, as you know, we set clear rules this morning. If you are caught with an unapproved book, there will be consequences." He crosses his arms and peers up at me from behind his bifocals. I make no effort

64

to speak because I'm afraid I'll cry. I'm not sure my voice would sound as brave as I want it to. And I can't apologize for reading. He can do whatever he wants. "You will attend detention after school today."

Except that. "But I have band practice!"

"Not today, you don't. Here," he says, handing me a red reflective vest. "You'll need this."

"For *what*?"

"School beautification. Congratulations, Ms. Harper. You just joined today's litter crew." The bell rings. He double-clicks his pen and frowns. "Now if I were you, I'd be on my best behavior. You'd better get to class."

★

I'm so busy fuming after school ends that Graham manages to corner me.

"June."

I put my flute in its case, pick up my bag, and start for the door.

He blocks my path. "Please. Let me explain."

"I'd rather not right now." My face says everything that needs to be said.

He takes a step toward me and holds out a dandelion. "June, I'm sorry I helped clean out the library. But I didn't have a choice. My mom insisted because she said it would be good for me."

Graham has a point. I don't think anyone has ever said no to his mom and lived.

He touches my arm. "I really am sorry. Talk to me. Please."

He's going to find out anyway. I had to tell my section and Mr. Ryman during band class, so it's just a matter of time before word gets around. "I have detention, okay?"

"For what?"

I look him square in the eye. "What do you think?"

He gapes at me. "Where did you get . . . you-know-what?"

Like I'd tell him anything after what he did. I don't have time for this.

Graham takes a measured breath. "I have no right to ask you this. I know that. But"—he scuffs his shoe against the floor—"I like you, June. A lot. And I want to hang out with you outside of school."

"I'm not allowed to date."

He grins. "You're not allowed to date *yet,* but you could be. Maybe if you stopped getting into trouble, your parents would be happy for you to spend time with someone"—he clears his throat—"older and wiser. They could meet me."

He really doesn't get it.

"Maybe you could stop reading those books for a little while."

Those books?

He quickly adds, "If you want, I mean . . . I just thought maybe we could, I don't know—" I smile before I realize what I'm doing. For the first time ever, Graham seems nervous.

But he still helped clean out the library, so I shrug. "I have to go."

"June," he says, reaching for my hand. "You need me around."

My stomach does that annoying flip and I pull my hand away. "Why? So you can help my parents throw out my books?"

He smiles and places the flower in my hand. "No. So I can catch you when you fall. I'm good at that, remember?"

I hurry out of the room and make it to detention just in time for Mr. Hawkins to check my name on the clipboard. One more minute, and I would've had it for tomorrow, too. There are a few other kids here. Some eighth-grade guy who keeps skipping class, and a sixth grader who I'm pretty sure is a thief. I drop my backpack into a seat near the front, away from his sticky fingers. Just in case.

The sound of the band warming up is muffled through the windows. I look down at my dandelion and imagine Graham marching with the trumpets. That's the guy I know. Not the one who throws out books.

"Okay, vests on!" Mr. Hawkins snaps me back to reality. "Everyone take a pair of gloves and a trash bag. Let's go!"

When we step outside the building, there are still kids waiting for rides. The band's warm-up tones change over to the *Jaws* theme.

"June, you're responsible for the bushes here at the front."

There are moving trucks parked by the door. I work slowly, stuffing empty cans and bottles into the trash. I wipe my forehead with my sleeve and catch a sixth grader on a bench staring. He looks away. My face grows hotter as more and more people stare.

Not being allowed to date could be the least of my problems. My friends' parents will probably think I'm a bad influence. That's what my parents would say if Emma had gotten busted today instead of me. And it would be forever before I'd be able to hang out with her again. I glance toward the band. I forgave Emma. Maybe I could give Graham another chance, too. It's not like any of this was his idea. But then, his parents might not let him date *me*. I force back a snicker. I'm a seventh-grade nobody who's never gotten in trouble a day in my life, and all of a sudden, I'm bad news.

The door opens. Parent after parent wheels a cartful of books out the front door and toward the moving trucks. It's the ultimate punishment. Nothing would bother me more than seeing Ms. Bradshaw's books disappear. Nothing.

After detention finally ends, I trudge back to my locker to swap out my English book for social studies homework. Between Mr. Beeler's office and talking to Graham, I didn't have time earlier. Nothing about today is right, but that seems to be the trend this month. I slam my locker shut before I even realize what I've done. The impact pops open the locker next to mine. I've got to get a grip. This isn't like me. I reach to close it but then stop.

Candy wrappers speckle the bottom of the locker, and

there are a few wadded-up balls of paper. There's nothing else. Not a notebook, not a textbook, not a single photograph. I smooth out one of the balls of paper. It's a page of notes with formulas all over it dated last year. The other one is a haiku about Mr. Beeler and the fish on his wall.

This is definitely unapproved reading material!

I've never seen anyone use this locker, but it has to belong to someone. Otherwise, they'd put one of those plastic tie locks on it. I shut the door behind me and set off down the hall.

New posters cover the main hall with phrases like COMMUNITY STRONG, PROTECT OUR CHILDREN, and STUDENTS FOR A MORAL FUTURE. The last one is signed by the Student Club for Appropriate Reading. I scan the hallway and then quickly rip it down.

I wander through the school, avoiding going home and facing my parents after detention, and once again, I find myself in front of the library. The CLOSED sign is finally gone, and the door is propped open. A gasp escapes my throat before I can stop it. If you remove two-thirds of the books in a library, it leaves a gaping hole—like lots of tiny asteroids have blasted out entire sections. I walk the perimeter and scan the shelves. Fiction took the biggest hit; the only books remaining are for much younger kids. The nonfiction section seems to be mainly intact. But I'll bet if I looked more closely, I'd find a chunk of those missing, too. If anyone needs to consult a set of encyclopedias from thirty years ago, though, they're all set.

Looking at those empty shelves drives it home.

I've lost.

"TWO ROADS DIVERGED"

"**H**oney, come on! The popcorn's ready!"

I stuff the last of my laundry into a drawer and take a look around before I turn out the light. It's only Friday, and everywhere I go, I see empty shelves. I feel the absence more deeply here, though. My bedroom has been gutted. Well, except for the book hidden under my nightstand, but no one needs to know about that. I flick off the light and feel my way through the darkness.

The last thing I want is a mother-daughter TV night after everything that happened, but Dad's at a client meeting in town, and it's not like I have anything better to do. It wasn't supposed to be so low-key, though. Kate's fall break is this weekend, but she's "too busy" to come home.

There are popcorn bowls on the coffee table, and next to them are three different kinds of seasoning. Cinnamon and sugar, cheese powder, and just plain salt. It's like a gourmet popcorn buffet, and I can't help but think Mom is trying to apologize. For Kate not being here. Or for taking my books. Or both? I crash on the couch, wrap myself in the throw, and go straight for the popcorn. "This is awesome!" I say through a mouthful of cinnamon sugar. Mom smiles and I decide to take advantage of her good mood.

"Hey, Mom?"

"Mmm?"

"Do you think maybe sometime, I don't know, I could hang out with Graham after school? When I'm not grounded?"

Her mouth settles into a straight line. "No dating. You know how we feel about that. You're not old enough."

"It wouldn't be a date date. Just friends going to the diner or something." Yes. That's right. Friends who hold hands.

"It's not a date?"

"Not a date."

She grabs a handful of popcorn. "When you're not grounded, you can go to the diner *if* other people go with you. That's the deal. If you go by yourself and we hear about it, you won't go to the diner again until you're eighteen."

Fine. Group date it is. "Thanks, Mom." Since my detention, I've come straight home, done my homework, and helped cook dinner. This is my reward for following the rules.

She nods and hits Play.

It's *Fuller House*. Her favorite. Right when the credits start, she prods me with her perfectly polished big toe. "Hey," she says. "I'm glad we're getting a TV night." Mom really seems happier now that everything has calmed down. At least, it has for her. Otherwise, she'd never let me watch TV while I'm grounded.

I smile back at her. "Me too."

Later that night in the darkness of my bedroom, I can't sleep. When I close my eyes, all I can see is Mom, happy. Movie night felt so normal. So much more *me* than I've felt lately. But before I can even relax into feeling better about my parents, my mind switches like someone has a TV remote for my brain. And suddenly it's Ms. Bradshaw's smile on the screen.

Will she get her job back? Is she thinking about me? Would she even want to work in a library without books? After the way the school treated her, I wouldn't be surprised if she hit the road and never looked back. That's what I'd do. It still gets me that the security guard escorted her out like a mall shoplifter. You can't come back from something like that. Not really. The rumor is that it's just an investigation, but when security kicks a teacher out in front of the student body, I'm pretty sure the verdict is already decided. Guilty.

But the question on auto-repeat in my head is whether she blames me.

I know what she'd say. "Be honest, groupie. Did you learn something from that book? Did it make you think about something in your own life? Did you love it?"

I'd nod and say yes.

She'd say, "Then I don't regret a thing, and neither should you."

Except she's not here, and I'd give anything to hear her say it.

★

I'm walking down the sidewalk to school on Tuesday when a car revs up behind me. It's the purr of Mrs. Whitmore's blue SUV. For just a second, I think Graham's mom is going to slow down and offer me a ride, but she doesn't. If anything, she speeds up. Graham places his palm against the passenger window as they barrel past me.

I really *am* a problem child. But if my mom can start to forgive me, so can Graham's. I was a rule follower for a lot longer than I've been a rule breaker.

At the corner of Maple and Willow, I go straight.

The leaves flutter overhead in brilliant shades of ruby, tangerine, and gold. It won't be long now before they start to fall. Even walking to school alone, I'm in a good mood. Mom let me use her Keurig this morning, and I have the most amazing tumbler of hot chocolate in my hand. With marshmallows.

The moment I step through the double doors, Graham runs over to me. "Careful! Hot chocolate!" I say. At least there's a lid on it. His woodsy body spray mingles with the smell of cocoa.

He hands me another dandelion. "What do you think? Can you forgive me?" he asks.

"Yes," I say, taking the dandelion and tucking it into my pocket so the top of the flower sticks out. "But if you throw away any more books, that's it."

He nods. "Fair enough. And," he adds, "are you ever going to be ungrounded? Because . . . I, um, I know this

76

guy who wants to spend time with you. If your family will let him."

He looks nervous again, and somehow just knowing he likes me enough to be nervous makes me feel brave. I smile up at him. "Want to try that cool and smooth thing again?"

He grins. *"Try?"*

"You know, if you have a question to ask me."

Graham leans closer. "Wanna go with me to get some burgers?"

I don't know what I was expecting, but that wasn't it.

"That's smooth?" I laugh.

He beams at me. "Yep. So when are we going?"

"When I'm not grounded anymore. Maybe next week, but it has to be a group thing."

"As long as you're there, I'm happy." He nods. "And you're not getting grounded again anytime soon, right?"

I shake my head. "Nope."

"You're awesome. I mean it, June." He grins.

He threads his fingers through mine, falling into step with me on the way to my locker. Oh my gosh, oh my gosh, oh my gosh. It's not dating. I can't get in trouble for hand-holding, right? I mean, who's going to tell my parents?

"Oh, I almost forgot." Graham's voice startles me out of my handholding freak-out. "I'm not supposed to say anything, but my parents said if I keep my grades up, I get wireless headphones."

"Wow. That sounds amazing." He's actually already told me that, but I don't want to ruin the moment by saying so.

Graham leans back next to my locker and fiddles with the buttons on my backpack while I flip through my combination. Within a few seconds my lock pops open, and I hoist out the science book, which weighs five tons. Graham reaches for my hand again, so I slam the door shut with my shoulder.

The empty locker next to it pops open and I push it shut as the familiar chimes ring out over the loudspeaker. "Students, I know you've all been asking questions about the reopening of the library." And Ms. Bradshaw. And your book policy.

I freeze. Maybe this whole mess can finally be over. Please let Ms. Bradshaw be back where she belongs.

"I would like to welcome you all to visit our library before classes start this morning and greet Ms. Morgan. She will take care of our library circulation desk for the time being. Thanks, and have a Dogwoodrific day!" The chimes play, ending the announcement.

A substitute? Like, for a few days? Or are we talking about something more permanent?

Graham kicks at the floor. "Guess she's not coming back just yet. Sorry." He brightens. "Want to go check it out?"

"I'll pass."

"Are you sure?"

I nod. I won't find anything I want in there. "So, on a scale of one to ten, how much damage have I done with your parents?"

He runs his free hand through the back of his hair. "Just give them some time. They won't stay mad forever."

"You sure about that? Association with me is damaging to the reputation."

He laughs. "Yes, because you are so deeply troubled."

"I'm serious. People love to talk. Everyone knows about my detention."

"Yeah, but you're not doing that stuff anymore, and that's all I care about."

That stuff. He talks about it like I've kicked a bad habit or something. I force a smile back at him.

He says, "Trust me." He releases my hand. "Now get in there and show everyone how wrong they are."

★

Emma barrels toward me moments after I leave science. *"June Harper!"* she squeals. "Tell me every. Single. Thing."

"About what?"

"Oh no you don't. You held hands with Graham in front of the whole world this morning. *Spill.*"

I laugh. "And where were you this morning, anyway?"

She flushes. "My mom heard about your detention and is giving me rides to school this week."

"Oh."

"Yeah. I'm sorry."

"Me too. It's weird walking to school without you."

"June. I love you, but stop stalling already and tell me everything!" Emma demands.

"Okay, okay! My mom said I can hang out with him— even at the diner—as long as I'm with a group."

"Finally!" She grabs my arm. "And then he held your hand?"

"Something like that."

"Wow. Wow, wow, wow. And then what?"

"He walked me to class. The end."

She shakes her head. "That's so not the end. This is the beginning! I'm going to find out how long he's liked you."

"What? Em, no, don't!"

"Too late, it's happening."

"What are you going to do?" I ask.

"It'll be fine. You'll see." Something tells me it won't be fine. Just like when she told me riding our bikes as fast as we could down Walnut Hill would be fine and I ended up with a faceful of dirt.

I groan.

"I can't believe it's finally here. How long have we talked about dating?"

"I've talked about it today. *You've* talked about it forever."

She loops her arm through mine as we walk into the art classroom. "Everything's going to change now. Just wait. It's going to be amazing."

★

After lunch, the library door is propped open. Out of curiosity, I peek inside. At first I think it's empty, but then I see a tuft of gray hair sticking up behind the back shelves.

"Hello?"

A throat clears. "Yes? I'm back here."

I follow the voice to the back. An older lady wearing a beige sweatshirt with ABCs all over it sits at a table eating a sandwich. Bright pink blush covers her pale cheeks.

"Hello, dear. Can I help you find something?"

Not likely. I twist my face into something pleasant anyway. It's not her fault Ms. Bradshaw is gone. "I was just wondering if you had anything new."

She frowns. "No, all shipments have been stopped. I don't think there will be any more for a while."

"Oh."

"Is there anything I can help you find?"

"No," I say. I look around at the empty shelves. "You don't have it."

She smiles. "Okay. Come back if you change your mind."

In English, it's "Goody" this and "Goody" that during our monotone read-through of *The Crucible*. I tune out for a bit after a girl accuses someone of being a witch and the whole town believes her. There's something wrong with that.

I focus on the illustrated poetry projects covering the walls in swirls of color. We just completed them last month, but it feels like forever ago.

Ms. Gibson cues me back to Earth. "What does this

tell us about the author's portrayal of accusations and fear-mongering? June, what are your thoughts?" She leans against her desk.

"He wanted to show how damaging they can be."

"Interesting. Why do you say so?"

"Because when you're in a small town, it doesn't matter what the judge says. The people living there are the ones who really make the call."

"In what way?" Ms. Gibson leans toward me, nodding. People turn in their seats to stare.

"Honestly? Because sometimes gossip weighs more than the truth."

Ms. Gibson raises her eyebrows. "Can you think of a real-life example?"

Don't say it. Abort! Abort! I shake my head. "I can't."

She frowns and moves on to someone else. It's like she's fishing for someone to blurt out, "Ms. Bradshaw!"

Where am I even living anymore? Dogwood or Salem? They look so much alike; it's as if we're stuck in the 1600s. And then I wonder if that's Ms. Gibson's point. *The Crucible* isn't even on the seventh-grade honors reading list, but she got special permission to teach it early when they restricted everything else. Maybe Ms. Gibson is on our side. I smile at the thought.

★

I go through the motions in band, but something feels off. Everyone saw me in the red vest for detention. And I can still feel people staring today. Graham tries to be reassuring, but it doesn't help.

Graham squeezes my hand a few minutes after the bell rings. "I'd give you a ride home," he says, "but it's probably not a good idea right now." Then he strolls out to his mom's SUV. Emma winks at me over her shoulder and follows him. *That's* what she meant? She's going to ask him about liking me in the car? *With his mom?* She doesn't need to do this. Why can't my best friend just walk home with me? Talk to *me* about him.

I kick a few pebbles scattered on the sidewalk as I walk home. Through the windows of the diner, kids from school are already drinking milk shakes. Brooke and a couple of flute players wave, their orders of curly fries and onion rings already on the table. My mouth waters.

As of tomorrow, I'm not grounded anymore. I'll be free—so to speak. I could go out with Graham, but it's probably too soon after my detention for his parents to be okay with that. I could read, but there's nothing left worth reading.

Freedom isn't very freeing after all.

Before long, I'm at the intersection of Willow and Maple Lane. I've got nothing else to do, so I might as well take the long way home. I look both ways and turn right on Maple. Light filters through the leaves, speckling my shoulders with warmth in the crisp air. I breathe it in, already feeling better.

But I didn't come here for the leaves.

A dog barks in the backyard of a nearby house. A few doors down from the dog is the Little Free Library. I look around. There's not a single kid my age anywhere.

I open the door. Today there are some old magazines and a copy of *Roll of Thunder, Hear My Cry*.

I don't think. I don't pause. I slip the novel into my bag and somehow make it home without my feet touching the ground. So what if I can't catch my breath right now? I caught a break instead. I shove the book under my nightstand and force myself to calm down. Time to act normal.

I have a healthy dinner with my parents. I eat all the right things and have just the right attitude, and when the moment is perfect, I tell them I have to go upstairs to read a play if I want to get into a good college.

Mom beams at Dad. They think they're responsible

for this change. They think everything worked according to plan, which is exactly what I want them to think.

Books are worth the risk.

I open *Roll of Thunder, Hear My Cry*. Another message is scrawled in blue ink.

> To Brendan,
> who once told me that
> family is everything.

I puzzle over the inscription. Who is Brendan, and why are his books circulating through the neighborhood? I tuck these questions away and lose myself in southern Mississippi, where I stay until I can't keep my eyes open.

RISK

The next morning, I approach the Little Free Library with something to trade. I slip my copy of *The Graveyard Book* into the box, and find *The Lightning Thief*.

I know there's something written in it before I even open the cover.

> To Brendan,
> whose greatest strength is within.

I've already read it, but I take it anyway. Farther down the street, I plop down on the curb and open my green notebook. Flipping to the back, I copy the inscriptions from *The Lightning Thief* and *Roll of Thunder, Hear My*

Cry. I also add what I remember of *The Secret Horses of Briar Hill.*

Mr. Beeler was quite clear in his office: *If you are caught with an unapproved book, there will be consequences.*

But what if nothing is found in my possession?

Rule number one: Don't get caught.

★

I duck in the side door to avoid the main lobby and Graham and Emma and go straight to my locker. Behind my gigantic social studies book, I engross myself in *Roll of Thunder, Hear My Cry* in the middle of the hallway. No one suspects anything if you do it in the open.

Someone stops right next to me. I remain perfectly still even as my stomach lurches forward. Please don't be Graham. *Please* don't be Graham.

"That's some heavy reading you've got there." Matt smiles down at me, his brown hair sweeping low into his eyes.

"History is important," I say.

"I've always thought so." He drops next to me on the cold linoleum floor. "What are you really reading?"

"You wouldn't be interested."

"Try me."

I flash him the cover of the novel.

He leans over to get a better look. "What's it about?"

"It's about this kid, Cassie, during the Depression. Her family has land, and a bunch of racist people think they shouldn't have it. I can't put it down because I'm so afraid something bad is going to happen." And I really love Cassie's family.

"Sounds serious." He settles back against the cinder block wall. "What else is it about?"

I flip through the pages, unsure of what to say. But he seems genuinely interested so I say, "It's about a whole bunch of other stuff that I'm still thinking about. Some of it is hard to read because it makes me so mad. I hate that people used to talk like that." Or treat people like that.

I don't know exactly what it is about him, but I trust him. So I say the words that have been stuck in my throat since this whole mess started. "All I know is, they don't want me to read it, so I'm gonna. Every last book I can find."

He laughs. "Who knew you were such a rebel?"

"I figure it's my mind. I'll read what I want to read."

Silence. His eyes follow me as I turn the page. I steady myself with a deep breath and wipe my sweaty palms on my pants.

"You got another one?"

I slip *The Lightning Thief* out of my bag behind the cover of my social studies book. "Understand you're taking a major risk." As am I. My pulse quickens. Better set some conditions first.

He raises an eyebrow and reaches for it.

I pull it back just out of his reach. "Ah-ah-ah! Hold on. Rule number one: Don't get caught. I mean it. Rule number two: Don't squeal. You just found this book. I had nothing to do with it. Rule three: Give it back to me when you're done. If you write in it, so help me, I will find you. Got it?"

He grins. "Do I get a library card?"

I groan. "No," I say, shoving my books into my bag for first period.

And then I stop.

A library.

★

"I hate painting. I wish they'd let me take study hall instead." Emma slides into her usual art table with a clean palette and looks at me a moment or two while I choose my colors. "Hello? Earth to June. Are you not talking to me?"

"Hi."

"All right. You're mad. Out with it."

I dilute my red paint with water until it pales, then dip my brush into it. "What makes you think I'm mad? You ditched me to ride home with Graham. Why would I be upset?"

"But June, I did that for *you*."

I roll my eyes.

"I did! Besides, you're *grounded*. I couldn't see or talk to you if I tried."

I stare at her until she squirms.

"I'm sorry! I know it's not your fault you're grounded. But my mom won't let me walk with you. At least for now," Emma says. "Ugh, this whole thing is awful. My parents gave me 'the talk' about what I'm allowed to read."

"Welcome to the club." I roll my eyes. "Also, I'm not grounded anymore."

"Good! As soon as my mom will let me, I'm gonna plan a sleepover just like old times. Bake cookies, a scary movie, the works!" Emma smiles at me hopefully.

"Yeah," I say. "But nothing too scary. You know we're not old enough for that!" I smirk and when Emma laughs it really does feel like old times.

She smears light blue paint over the first layer, but

the darker color peeks through. "So did you oversleep this morning?" she asks.

"No, why?"

"Because you didn't hang out with me before school! I thought about checking the library . . . but I was pretty sure you wouldn't be there. Where were you?"

"Yeah, definitely not in the library. I . . ." I'm not sure I'm ready to tell Emma about the Little Free Library. Or sharing my books with Matt. So I just say, "I took the long way to school. You know how I love when the leaves change!" To prove my point, I layer another coat of pale, watery red onto the leaves on my canvas.

Emma nods. "Well, I missed you," she says.

"Me too."

Mr. Garcia walks over and says, "Nice work, June."

I sigh and put down my paintbrush. "It just seems like no matter how much I do, nothing changes."

"But it *is* changing."

No, it isn't. What I'd like to do is throw my canvas out the window, but then I'd fail art.

"I know you can't see it right now, but every time you add a layer, it deepens the pigment." His thumb strokes his beard. "You know what, June? If you don't believe me, I'll let you see for yourself." He strolls up to the front of the room and digs around in a drawer. He returns with a camera. "Here. You do the honors. We'll take another one in a week so you can see the difference."

I go along with it and snap a photo of my painting. "Wouldn't it be a whole lot faster if I painted with a deeper color?"

He reaches for the camera. "You could, but then you'd ruin it."

"Ruin it?"

"You'd be missing all the layers." He smiles. "That's what makes it beautiful."

★

I have to wait until lunch to visit my locker. I'm not supposed to be in the hallway then because teachers aren't around, and that's exactly why this is my moment.

I open locker 319, next to mine. It doesn't have a combination lock, so all I have to do is lift the lever out of place. Nothing has changed since the last time I looked inside, but somehow, it looks totally different. Full of promise. I crumple the trash in my hand and toss it into the hallway bin.

I dart a glance down the hall.

No one.

I retrieve *Roll of Thunder, Hear My Cry* from my bag and place it on the bottom shelf of the locker with the spine out. It looks cavernous and pitiful with just one book.

One book can change everything.

I know where I can get more.

★

The next day, I get up earlier than usual. I have somewhere I need to be. Maple Lane. Today's selections include *Diary of a Wimpy Kid, Because of Winn-Dixie,* and the first Harry Potter book. *The Graveyard Book* is still where I left it. Right as I gather the new books in my arms, I see a flicker of movement at the blinds in the window. I freeze.

I wish I had something to share so I wouldn't feel so bad about walking off with their books. Next time.

As soon as I make my way to the curve in the road, I plop down next to a random mailbox. I pull out my green notebook, flip to the inscription page, and open the Harry Potter book. *To Brendan, because love is the greatest power of all.* In *Because of Winn-Dixie,* it's *To Brendan, who knows the magic of a summer storm.* And in *Diary of a Wimpy Kid*, it's *To Brendan, who's always known that popularity isn't everything.*

I copy all the inscriptions into my notebook. Why these books? And what happened to Brendan? I turn past my English doodles to the second page and write *Inventory* at the top. Then I list all the books I've gotten. I draw a line through *The Secret Horses of Briar Hill.* It's a loss.

When I reach campus, I duck in the side door again so I can hide while I read. I feel a twinge of guilt about not hanging out with Emma, but that doesn't stop me from diving into the Harry Potter book the moment I find a quiet spot. I was never allowed to read the books or see the movies, but I've always wanted to.

I'm just learning about mail delivered by owls when Matt slides next to me on the floor.

"That must be the most interesting textbook in the world."

"You have *no* idea."

He tilts his head toward mine. "What are you really reading?"

I flash the cover toward him.

"Oh yeah! My cousin loves those."

"How old is your cousin?"

"Ten."

Perfect. There are ten-year-olds who are allowed to read more than I am. "Did you finish *The Lightning Thief*?"

"Yeah." He retrieves it from his bag and slips it to me under my textbook.

"And?"

He shoots me a dazzling smile. "Two thumbs up. What else ya got?"

I pass him *Diary of a Wimpy Kid*.

He nods and tucks it away. "Actually, can I keep *The Lightning Thief* for my friend Abby?" Off my expression, he quickly adds, "She's in eighth grade, and believe me, she won't say a word."

"Abby Rodriguez?" I've seen her in the band room a few times. She's always wearing Vans and cool T-shirts.

"Yeah. She's so ticked over what they did to the library. You'd like her."

I don't have a problem with sharing, but I don't know anything about her except she's infinitely cooler than I am. "Same rules apply for her, too. Got it?"

"Yes, ma'am."

He'd better be sure about her. I slip the book back to

him and then flip to a blank page in the middle of the green notebook. I write LOANS at the top. "I'm going to use code names to keep track of everything. You know, just in case. What do you want yours to be?"

"Batman."

I laugh. "Batman?"

"Always be yourself, unless you can be Batman. Then be Batman."

"Batman it is." Number one on the list is *Batman, Diary of a Wimpy Kid.*

He leans over and studies the page. "What's yours going to be?"

"Supergirl."

He tilts his head. "Not Wonder Woman? She has that awesome golden lasso."

"Supergirl can *fly.*" In Abby's slot for number two, I write *Wonder Woman, The Lightning Thief.*

"This is true." Matt absentmindedly taps a folded piece of paper against his knee.

"What's that?"

"They were handing them out at the front door." He hands it to me.

In bold letters, it reads:

REMINDER FOR STUDENTS

Texts containing profanity, drugs, violence, rock/rap music, witchcraft, drinking, smoking, or rebellion of any kind are BANNED.

Any student caught with a banned book will face serious consequences.

"Rebellion of any kind," I say. "What do you think they mean by that?"

"Hard to say. Like some kind of protest? I don't know." He leans his head against the wall.

I rifle through the front pocket of my bag until my fingers close around my black Sharpie. In big, messy letters, I write on the cover of my notebook:

PROPERTY OF THE REBEL LIBRARIAN

Matt laughs. "Look at you, all bad in your cardigan."

I smile sweetly. "You have no idea." The words tumble out of my mouth like I'm always this bold.

He nods at the notebook. "I should've known from your handwriting. It looks like a serial killer's."

"Bad handwriting is a sign of brilliance." Mom

wouldn't say the same, though. She hates my writing with the fire of a thousand suns. Last year she wouldn't even let me help address Christmas cards. I slip the notebook back into my bag and weigh the flyer and my words carefully. "Hey—my friends are going to think something's up if I don't start coming in the front door again." Actually, they've already noticed.

He nods like he's not at all surprised. "You mean Graham's going to wonder where you are."

My cheeks grow hot. "Just meet me at locker 319 tomorrow, okay?"

"When?"

"During class change, but only if Graham and the flutes aren't there. Otherwise, keep walking."

"Why not include him?"

I search for the right words. "I'm not sure he'd understand."

Matt nods. "Mind if I bring other people?"

My stomach does a little flip. Who does he want to bring? Will they rat me out the first chance they get? I steel my nerves. Matt wouldn't bring them if he thought that. He's in this, too. "Sure. Bring whoever you want, but *only* if they can follow the rules." I hand him the flyer. "I don't want to get busted because you trusted the wrong person."

He smiles. "May we never get caught."

I nod and walk away, my cheeks still pink. He makes it sound as though we're vandalizing the hallway or cheating on a test, when we're really just a couple of kids reading books.

But as I walk into the main hall papered in new flyers, it's clear. What we're doing is much, much bigger.

LOCKER 319

After art, I swing by my locker. Matt, Abby, and Colby, another eighth grader, lean casually against the wall like they own it. Graham is nowhere in sight.

"Hi, June," Colby says, his green eyes and fair skin peeking out from under a mop of floppy red hair.

"Hey!" I smile at him and turn to Abby. "I'm June."

Abby grins. Today she's rocking a nineties band shirt with leggings, a skirt, and short boots. "I know who you are." I think that's the first time in my life anyone has ever said that to me. Abby brushes one of her dark waves from her face, exposing brown eyes and brown skin. People with perfect hair baffle me. I'd need a salon miracle to make mine do that.

I glance up and down the hallway; then I open the locker a few inches to reveal *Roll of Thunder, Hear My Cry* and *Because of Winn-Dixie*. "Take your pick. I wish I had more."

She swaps *The Lightning Thief* for *Roll of Thunder, Hear My Cry*. "I guess you're our new Ms. Bradshaw, huh?" she asks.

I smile at the thought but shake my head. "Nobody could replace her."

Abby nods. "Yeah, I miss being one of her groupies."

"You are—were—a groupie?" I ask.

"Yup! I used to swing by after sixth period every time I needed a new book," Abby says. That must be why I don't know her better. I was more of a morning groupie because of after-school band practice.

"Speaking of new books, can I take one?" Colby asks. I move to the side so he can grab *Because of Winn-Dixie*. "Thanks, June." I saw Colby every week this summer when my mom dragged me with her to the grocery store to buy organic vegetables. His family owns the store, so he spent the summer bagging groceries there. He's always been nice to me.

I scribble down their code names and the books they're borrowing. "I have some ground rules—"

"We know," Colby says. "Matt told us."

I nod at Matt.

"Hey, I have a few books stashed in my closet," Abby says. "You want me to bring them?"

"Yeah, that would be great. Thanks. I'll make sure they stay in good shape," I promise.

"Keep them. Just bring more books."

"Done." Maybe I can share a few with the Little Free Library after taking so many. I close the locker.

"I'll meet you here tomorrow morning—"

"Only if she's alone," Matt says.

Abby dismisses him with a wave. "We know, we know."

I pause for a moment and then remove the combination lock from my own locker. One flip and a click later, locker 319 is secure.

★

Graham halfheartedly loads up his lunch tray. "Are you avoiding me?" he asks while we stand in the lunch line.

"No." If I were avoiding him, I wouldn't even go to the cafeteria. I'm only in line because I forgot to bring a drink to go with my lunch.

"I don't see you in the mornings anymore." His tone is accusing.

"Some of us have to walk."

He ladles fat-free cheese onto his whole-wheat tortilla chips. At least, I think they're whole-wheat. Could be baked cardboard. Who can tell? He picks up his tray and doesn't speak.

I can't share my library with him. Not after he begged me to give the books a rest so I wouldn't be grounded forever. I'm still thinking about what to say when he touches my arm and says, "It's just—I miss seeing you."

Graham's forehead wrinkles. He's waiting for me to say it back, but the words won't come. So I say the truth. "It's been a while."

He grabs a carton of milk and types in his lunch code at the register. "It has. But that's not my fault."

"It's not mine, either," I say. But I guess it kind of is. Just not for the reason he thinks.

He shrugs. "Whatever, June."

★

"Back to one, people. Let's go," Mr. Ryman's voice barks over the loudspeaker.

I stand in place by Emma while everyone else scatters to their spots.

Matt lightly bumps into me as he runs by. "Whoops! Sorry, Ms. Harper." He winks. I don't have to imagine the look on Emma's face. I can see her dumbstruck expression in the corner of my eye. This is going to be bad.

By the end of the routine, Emma's jaw is set in a hard line. She darts by me faster than I've ever seen her move.

"Hey!" I call after her.

She doesn't respond.

"Emma! Wait!"

She whirls around, lips pressed flat and her pulse thudding in the vein at her temple. "I hate what you're doing to Graham. It makes me sick."

I make a conscious effort not to let my mouth drop open. It's not easy. "And what, exactly, am I doing to Graham?"

"You've got this amazing guy who's trying to get to know you, and it's like you just don't care. You've been avoiding him every day. And don't think I don't see how you're looking at Matt."

"Matt's my friend—"

"Since *when*?" She perches a hand on each hip, staring me down. "You *know* I like him."

I stop at that. Why haven't I told Emma about Matt?

The library is a secret, but Matt doesn't need to be. I sigh, unsure of what to say.

"Why would he even talk to you?" Emma snaps.

In all the years I've known Emma, I've never seen her like this. Not with me, anyway. "Look, we stayed after school once, and now we say hi when we see each other. That's it." Which is mostly true. "Believe me, I'd never do that to you." Which is completely true.

Her expression doesn't change.

My heart starts racing. I can't stop the words from tumbling out of my mouth. "And what have you been doing? Hanging out with the guy who's trying to get to know me."

Her eyes widen the tiniest bit.

I manage to look her square in the eye. "It's more than just riding home from school with him, isn't it?"

For the first time ever, Emma is silent.

The lump forming in my throat makes it hard to speak. "So what's wrong here, Em? What I'm doing to Graham? Or what you're doing to—" My voice cracks. "Me."

She doesn't look the least bit sorry. Just mad. "Are you done?"

I flinch. "Yeah. We're done."

Normally, I'd read to distract myself from a fight with Emma. Not that we've ever fought like this. But since I still can't read out in the open at home, I decide to work on the library. I need to figure out how to transport books without getting busted. I saw this movie once where people hid stuff in drawers with false bottoms. I need that, but in my backpack. Something like a concealed layer.

"Mom, I'm home!" I toss my keys onto the side table.

There's no response over the instrumental album she found at a yard sale. It helps her channel her artistic spirit, or so she says.

I sprint up the stairs and find her tucked away in her studio. She's always working on a new art project of some kind. Pink pastel cozies for the toilet paper rolls in every bathroom. Latch-hook wall hangings. Today, she's hunched over a canvas and stippling white paint on tree branches against a black sky. Perfect. I've never been so happy to see her focused on her art. Because that means I stand a chance of not getting caught.

"Mind if I use your sewing machine?" I ask.

She glances up from the painting. "Nope. Need some help?"

"I'm good." *Be natural. Casual.* "Hey, do you still have

the black vinyl from when you made that raincoat for Mrs. Collins's dog?"

"Why?"

I shrug. "Oh, I've just been thinking about all the money you put into my flute, and I thought it would be good to create a waterproof bag to protect it." I'll be her favorite before Christmas if I keep this up.

Mom beams at me. "That's a brilliant idea." I feel a twinge of guilt at that. But I stay focused on my task. She taps her brush against the palette. "You know, I think there's a scrap or two, but not much. You might get a few feet out of it."

"How about black Velcro?"

"In the odds-and-ends basket. It's next to the sewing machine in Kate's room. Help yourself." Mom wanted more room for her art supplies, so she moved her sewing stuff in there when Kate started school. I thought Kate would be upset, but you have to come home to find out about things like that.

"Perfect!"

"Sure you don't need help?"

"Nah, I want to try it by myself." I turn to go to Kate's room.

"Hey, June?"

I pause and look over my shoulder. "Yeah?"

Her face practically glows with happiness. "I'm so proud of you. You're really showing us how much you've grown."

I smile back at her. With each step I take down the hall, I shrink an inch.

But there's no time to lose. Not even to look around at all the things my sister left behind and feel like one of them. First, I measure the bottom of my bag. With Mom's fabric scissors, I cut a rectangular piece of material an inch bigger all around and stitch the fuzzy side of black Velcro around the border with black thread. Now comes the hard part. I flip my backpack inside out. At about three inches above the bottom of the bag, I stitch the prickly Velcro around the sides in a crooked horizontal line. I use purple thread to match my bag, of course. It looks okay, but I'd never make it as a seamstress.

Almost time to test it. I flip the bag right side out and scoot it to the floor.

Mom strides in with paint smears on her arms. "How's it going?" She reaches for the sturdy black rectangle and folds it over. The creases around her mouth deepen. "I hate to tell you, but the Velcro won't stick like this. The pieces should be opposites."

"Oh no. I knew something was off." I let my shoulders fall.

"You'll get there. Holler if you need me." She pads back down the hall to her easel.

I align the material with the Velcro strip inside the bag and press gently around the edges. I can't believe it—it actually looks like a normal bottom. Now for the test. I add my textbooks, and their weight presses down on the fabric. With books under the layer to support the load, it just might work.

Mom calls, "Already done?"

"Nah. I threw it out," I yell back. "I'll just use a big freezer bag if it rains."

"Oh, that's clever," she says. It was also my plan all along.

I zip my updated bag. "Thanks!"

★

The next morning, cinnamon toast and hard-boiled eggs await me in the kitchen alongside a thermos of hot chocolate. The saliva pools in my mouth. I haven't eaten like this in weeks. Months, really. We stopped having family breakfasts when Kate left. I don't know why. One day we ate together, and the next, we didn't. It just happened.

"What's all this?"

Mom pulls a plate from the hot, soapy water in the sink. "Oh, I got up early today and thought you needed something better than a breakfast bar."

"Thanks." This is one of her pride payments. She's proud of me, so I get the grand spread. Luckily, cinnamon toast still tastes good even when you don't really deserve it.

"You want a ride?" She scans my outfit from head to toe and then looks back up at me, pleased. I'm wearing a long dusty-blue shirt with skinny jeans and ballet flats. The picture of innocence.

"No thanks, I'll walk. It's so beautiful outside."

She smiles. "Suit yourself. Now go learn something."

At least that's an order I can obey. Just not exactly the way she means. I take Maple Lane to school. This time I survey the blinds in the window before I touch a single novel, but there's no trace of movement. That's too bad, because I'd like to meet the person behind this library. Inside the box, I find:

The Witches

George

The first Dork Diaries book

Brown Girl Dreaming

I wish I had my notebook, but I decided to make it part of locker 319. Less to get caught with that way. On a loose piece of paper, I scribble the titles and inscriptions— these books, like the other ones, include messages to Brendan. The books stack perfectly along the bottom of my backpack, and there's still enough space for the Velcro to seal it off from the main compartment. With my textbooks on top, it looks like a normal bag.

It works!

I walk into school a changed person. My heart beats a little faster, and there's a goofy grin on my face. This feels so right.

Graham loops his arm through mine. "I'm sorry," he says. I breathe in the smell of him. I can't help it. But I freeze midsniff. The scent of peaches is fused with his woodsy body spray. I clench my jaw. "Glad you're finally here," he says, pulling away and smiling down at me. A shiny Student Club for Appropriate Reading button glints from his shirt pocket. Wow. His mom might have made him help clear out the library, but this? This is all Graham. And I am so done with him.

I'm going to tell him what I really think, and it's going to be awesome. I am. But right now I just need him out of my way. If you'd told me two months ago that I'd be avoiding *him*, I wouldn't have believed it.

He shrugs. "I'm going to grab some breakfast. You want anything?"

"I already ate."

"Okay. Be back in ten minutes?"

I smile. "Sure. That should do it." In the time it takes him to stuff his face, I can distribute banned books to four people.

But when I round the corner, there are at least eight kids standing by my locker. They can't all be waiting for me, can they?

Abby is front and center. Today she wears a different nineties rock band shirt and carries a tote bag that says I'D RATHER BE READING. The graphic is a colorful stack of books with an outline of a heart stenciled around it.

I snort. "Nice bag."

"I thought it was appropriate." She winks.

It's like the world's best camouflage. Flaunt it in the open and no one cares. I slip my bag from my shoulders. "Um, so, are you all here to see me?"

Matt smiles. If this keeps up, I'll need to set up a table in the hallway.

I'm only one digit away from unlocking locker 319 when Abby plants her elbow across the frame. Before I can comment, Mr. Beeler rounds the corner, walkie-talkie in hand. "Good morning," he calls out as he passes.

This is how it all ends. Right now, surrounded by accomplices and books. I casually wipe my sweaty palms across my jeans.

Mr. Beeler fiddles with a knob on his walkie-talkie, and then he's gone. No questions. No stares. Mom always says there's safety in numbers. Guess she's right. We're just hanging out before school—me and the kids I used to think were too cool to even talk to me. My life is getting weirder by the second.

Abby steps away from the locker. "Well, that was close."

"How did you know he was coming? The dude crept in like a ninja." I pop open the locker.

She shrugs a shoulder. "Static on his radio. Dead giveaway."

I'm impressed. I'd never thought about that before. Then again, I've never really needed to be on the lookout for adults until now. "Here," I say, handing the notebook to Matt. "Have them write down their code names. We'll list the books they choose in a minute."

"Sure thing, Supergirl." My cheeks flush a little when he says it.

Kneeling down, I lift the compartment cover and scan the hallway. I balance the bag on my knee and use it to block my locker while I transfer the books to the shelf. Not unlike, I realize with a twinge of guilt, the way Ms. Bradshaw used to do it. But she could do it out in the open.

Abby slips me three of her books at a time. *A Snicker of Magic, Doll Bones, Blubber.*

I hold up the last one partly because it used to be on my shelf but mostly because I'm thrilled another person has read it, too.

Abby shrugs. "I love Judy Blume."

I nod. "I read *Tales of a Fourth Grade Nothing* until it fell apart."

This week is blowing my mind. I don't think I've ever said two words to Abby or vice versa before now, and here we are talking about our favorite books when no one wants us to.

The next handful includes *Bridge to Terabithia, Better Nate Than Ever,* and *Number the Stars.*

And then finally, *Wolf Hollow,* three Goosebumps books, and *Pax.*

I'm in heaven. I haven't read half of these, but it would be selfish to hold them all for myself.

"The books I've been bringing in . . . I sort of need to replace them—like a trade. Are you cool if I use a couple of these for that?"

"Sure," Abby says. "It's all about sharing, right?"

I nod and stuff a few into my bag to add to the Little Free Library later. "Thanks, these are great." I glance at the surrounding lockers. To their credit, everyone waiting in line looks like they're doing normal things before school starts. They're talking about my rules, messing with backpacks, putting on ChapStick, and, of course, passing around my notebook. Matt leans back casually, his right foot pressed against the locker. To anyone passing by, he looks like a random kid. To me, he's a lookout.

"Incoming," Abby whispers, and completely turns her back to me.

I scan the hallway for the principal, but all I see is Graham striding to my locker, stuffing the last of his biscuit into his mouth. "Sorry," he says. "The line took forever."

Matt and Colby give a nod to Graham as they stroll to the opposite end of the hallway.

Graham looks around and tosses the biscuit wrapper into the trash. "What's with all the people?"

I shrug. "There's no more than usual."

Graham puts his arm around me. "You won't have to compete with the crowd much longer. Promise. You'll be here plenty early when you ride to school with me." He hefts my bag to his shoulder. "What do you have in here? Bricks?"

My mouth twitches. "Textbooks."

Olivia nods at me as we pass by her. Does she know? All I need is for someone to ask about my locker right now, and it will be over before it even starts.

But no one asks for books. No one even glances my way. Graham takes my hand in his, and I fight the impulse to snatch it away. My stomach is definitely not getting that flippy feeling anymore.

Matt leans over the water fountain, then draws himself to his full height moments before we pass. As he wipes his mouth with the back of his sleeve, his eyes meet mine. And then they flit down to my hand in Graham's.

His expression darkens. Then it's gone, like a cloud that blows across the sun so fast, you wonder if the shadow ever fell at all.

CHANGES

I don't think much of it when the sign in the grocery store window reads SOLD OUT OF FLASHLIGHTS. There's limited inventory in our town. It happens.

When I get to school, entire groups of kids stop what they're doing and smile at me when I walk by. Like, they're talking and laughing one second, and the next, there's a total silence that says *That's her*.

A few trail after me to my locker and make requests. A sixth grader asks, "Hey, June? I really need *EngiNerds*. I just finished my last Wimpy Kid book by flashlight last night."

I pause, then smirk. "Flashlight, huh?"

"Yeah," she says with a shrug. "How else am I going to stay up reading past my bedtime?"

Everywhere I look, kids line the hallways with over-sized textbooks in their laps. At lunchtime and after school, their sneakers dangle off sidewalk benches. I don't have to look to see what they're doing. I already know.

Reading.

And then I'm walking along, minding my own business, when Dan Fuller, the most popular guy in school, high-fives me in the lobby. My mouth gapes open as he walks away.

That's when I realize something has changed.

This is no longer the same Dogwood Middle. It's an alternate reality where reading is the coolest thing you can do and I, June Harper, am the leader of the cool kids—of the rebellion. I'm sure I'll wake up any minute now and everything will be back to the way it used to be.

But it doesn't end the next day. Or the next. Or the day after that.

I start to trust it, which is my first mistake.

ULTIMATUM

Dad strolls through the hall on his way to the PTSA meeting after band practice. I, of course, volunteered to put up appropriate-reading posters above the office doors. It's what good kids do.

"Make sure it's straight," he says. He beams at me.

"You got it, Dad." I'm back to being the good kid he wants me to be, and weirdly, it's starting to feel normal living this double life.

It's quiet after he leaves. I wander over to the drink machine, buy a diet soda (no sugar in these machines, thank you very much), and crack it open on the bench. I just can't get over the change in the lobby. There's a picture of a homeless kid on a street corner smoking and drinking beer. Below it, it says DO YOU KNOW WHAT YOUR KIDS ARE READING?

I choke, sending fizz sputtering out my nose like liquid fire. Who came up with this? There isn't even a book in the picture.

The next one reads THEY'RE BANNED FOR A REASON. It's signed by the Student Club for Appropriate Reading. SCAR. I groan. These posters just keep getting worse. How old do you have to be to read what you want? That magical age might as well be a YOU MUST BE THIS TALL TO RIDE sign at a carnival.

"You're a liar," says a soft voice to my left. One I'd recognize anywhere. Graham.

I whip my head to face him. "Excuse me?"

"You heard me." He slides into the seat next to me.

"Is this your idea of a joke? I don't get it."

Daylight filters in through the window and reflects off the SCAR button on his shirt. "June, *I know.*"

My eye twitches. Nobody ratted me out, or they'd have had to tell on themselves in the process. He can't know everything. There has to be something else I did to make him look so smug.

I take a slow sip of my drink and try to stay calm. "I have no idea what you're talking about."

"Maybe I should walk you to your locker. Help you carry your books. You have *so many* these days."

My heart beats faster. Stay calm. He might not know everything. If he did, wouldn't he have blabbed by now? The boy can't keep a secret to save his life. I, on the other hand . . . "I can manage. Thanks, though."

"You said you wouldn't." He actually looks a little hurt.

"I tried." I give a one-shouldered shrug. "But I can't."

"Can't?" His voice wavers with fury. "Or won't? Not that it matters anymore. June, you may not care about your life, but I care about mine." He shakes his head. "How do you think it looks when—did you ever stop to think about me?" Graham leans back into the seat. "I don't get it. I asked you not to sneak around so maybe, just maybe, we could spend some time together, and what do you do? You read every banned book you can find!"

He doesn't know about the locker! But he knows enough. I twist the tab on my soda can. I should've ditched him sooner. Now that he knows I'm still reading, anything could happen.

"Is all this just to get back at me?"

There are so many things wrong with what he just said that I don't even know where to begin. "Yes, I spent *hours* planning this as payback after I saw you dumping books out of the library. You know me so well."

His eyes narrow.

"Please. I couldn't stop reading, but you know what? I'm not the only one. Kind of awesome, right?"

He looks at me as if he's never seen me before. "I can't have this."

"You *can't have this*?" I shake my head. "What are you, my dad?"

"I mean it, June. I'll make it simple for you. Choose: books or me."

Dust motes float between us, filling the gap just made larger by his words. The tightness in my chest builds with each passing second. All I can do is stare at him, and he doesn't bother looking away, because he's not embarrassed. It hits me then—if he cared about me at all, he wouldn't talk to me like this. I take a breath. "You just chose for us."

I jump to my feet and take two whopping steps away before I freeze. He's not really choosing. I had already chosen. I whirl back around. "What's the matter with you? Reading books isn't wrong. I'll tell you what wrong is—it's trying to control someone."

His cheeks flush ever so slightly. "That's what you think I'm doing?"

"Yes! You're"—I scan the wall for just the right warning phrase—"well, there's not a poster for that one. Someone call the PTSA!"

"That's not fair."

I crumple my soda can. It makes me feel a whole lot stronger than I am. "My point exactly. It's not. And I'm done answering your questions."

He stands and shoves his hands in his pockets. "I'll question you if I want."

"Or what? Are you going to rat me out?"

Graham says, "I don't care about you or your books."

My heart is going to hammer out of my chest. I take a few deep breaths. When the words come, my tone is deadly. "You know, you say you 'can't have this,' but you're wrong about that. You can't have *me*. I don't even like you anymore."

Graham's shoulders slump a fraction. He doesn't look nearly as confident as he did a moment ago. "If you end this, we're over for good. I mean it. There's no going back."

I look deep into his blue eyes and slowly close the space between us. His apple Jolly Rancher breath catches and gusts in a warm burst across my skin. I lean in close, my voice soft in his ear. "I'll make it simple for you. I. Choose. Books."

NEW LEAF

After the PTSA meeting, I lean against the cool metal door of Dad's car. The smell of burning leaves is crisp, smoky, comforting. It brings me back to memories of hayrides with Kate. Marshmallows. Hot chocolate. Easier times before I realized just how strict my parents could be. Before I had a reason to notice. Maybe because they had two kids to focus on? This—all of this, the library, secrets, Graham, Emma—it would all feel so much easier if I had my sister to talk to.

Dad emerges with a manila envelope tucked under his arm. "Hey, kiddo."

He slides into the seat and tunes the radio to the oldies station. Thankfully, I've had years of practice tuning it out.

"And now," the announcer says, "an update on the controversy at Dogwood Middle.

"Parents are demanding answers as to why Natalie Bradshaw, the librarian whose actions sparked the movement against inappropriate books, is still employed by Dogwood Schools. The superintendent did not immediately respond to requests for comment."

Dad pushes the power button on the radio. "I heard you and Garrett Whitmore are getting close."

"It's Graham. And no, we're not."

"You sure about that?"

"Yeah," I say. "Not happening."

I sneak a glance toward the driver's side. Dad's face is smooth and expressionless, not revealing the slightest hint of a storm brewing below the surface. He turns on his blinker and eases onto Willow.

"You don't have anything to worry about," I say.

He leans back in his seat. Less than two minutes until we're home. "You know we have our reasons for not letting you date, right?"

I nod. Yes. I'm too young. Got it.

"Do I need to have a chat with his mom?"

I whip my head to the side. "Dad!" I can't read his face, which is still just as calm as ever. "No! You can't do that. You'd ruin my life." If he only knew how serious I am.

It's super-fast, but I think I catch the ghost of a smile flickering across his lips.

★

The next morning, *Holes* is waiting in the Little Free Library. Ms. Bradshaw said I'd like it. It's about a kid who's cursed with bad luck.

I flip to the first few pages. There's the message in blue ink:

To Brendan,
There's nothing that can't be fixed.

Something flutters at the edge of the window of the house just as I tuck the book away in my bag. Someone saw me. I'm sure of it. I slip *Escape from Mr. Lemoncello's Library* into the box and grin. They *have* to like that one if they have a Little Free Library in their yard.

I mull over the note in *Holes*. How do I fix a problem this big? My library is the only way I can fight back, but if the wrong people found out, everything would disappear.

Graham got close enough. I can only imagine what would happen if he figured out I'm running a library. They'd take my books, I'd probably be expelled, and my family would kill me.

Locker 319 has to stay a secret.

★

The air in the building is electric today, as if left over from last night's storm. I don't know what's causing more of a stir: the kids packing the hallway leading to my locker, or Graham and Emma snuggled up on a bench with their arms around each other.

My stomach lurches in a nausea dance.

As if he senses my presence, Graham glances right at me over Emma's shoulder. I don't even flinch. I look back at him like, *Oh, wow, look what YOU did*. This is a demonstration, a show, a rebound meant to make me cry, which doesn't make any sense at all. You have to lose something meaningful to cry. He doesn't get it at all. I'm not upset about losing *him*. I'm upset about Emma.

A light tap on my shoulder draws me away from the train wreck of my social life. "Hey," a sixth grader I haven't met before says. "June?"

I nod. "Yeah."

He runs his hand through his brown hair. "Do you have any Captain Underpants books?"

I grin. "Nope. Not yet."

"It's not for me," he adds. "My little brother loves those books, but his school said they weren't good for kids. I was hoping you might have it."

"You're kidding, right?" What's so wrong with a superhero saving the day in his underwear? It's not going to make kids refuse to put on pants or anything.

He shakes his head.

"I've read those—what did the school think is wrong with them?"

"They said they were offensive and couldn't believe something with *underpants* in the title was in the school library."

I shake my head. "Oh no, not *underpants*! I do declare, what happened to decency?" I motion for him to follow. "They need to get a life. Seriously."

He frowns across the lobby at Graham. "Yeah, that's a bit much right after breakfast," he says.

"Oh, I was talking about the elementary school," I say. "But I see your point."

Last year Emma borrowed my favorite white shirt, the gauzy one that made me feel as though I were floating, and dumped a whole glass of grape juice on it. Not on purpose, of course. She tried and tried to get the stain out, but it took hold of the fabric as if it had always been there. Nothing she did could fix it. She apologized for weeks afterward, and even though I told her it was okay, she still felt bad because she knew how much I loved it.

I guess guys are different from shirts.

Emma doesn't speak to me when I get to art class because she doesn't have to. Her face says it all.

She won.

I lost.

The girl who stained my shirt is long gone.

I think she sees the hurt on my face, because she smirks as she smears yellow acrylic paint over her sketch of a lopsided banana.

Mr. Garcia pulls up a chair next to her. "Emma, what's your composition?"

Her brush hovers in the air. The smile drains from her face. "Uh, I don't know yet. I'm still figuring it out."

His thumb grazes his beard. "It's already there if you look for it. What do you see?"

Now Emma looks annoyed. I stare at my brush-strokes and try to control the smile that curls at my lips.

She narrows her eyes. "Fruit?"

"Look closer," he says. He gestures to the curve of the bowl, the lines of the banana, the slant of the pear. "See that? It's a circle. In your composition, everything is connected. What seems to be the end is the beginning, and the beginning is actually the end."

That's one way of looking at it. Her beginning with Graham is actually the end with me. I swallow a lump that's worked its way into my throat.

Her brows furrow. "I only see fruit."

"I think I see the composition in mine," I say.

It's like Mr. Garcia has a new purpose, the way his face lights up. "Oh? Show me."

I gesture to the lines of the main branches of my maple tree and the places where they intersect. "I see a triangle here. There are two points at the bottom, and the third one"—I indicate the uppermost leaf—"is at the top."

Emma rolls her eyes.

Mr. Garcia beams at me. "You're a natural, Ms. Harper."

He glances at the photo propped up by my painting. "Can you see how much your work has changed?"

"Yeah. It's just boring to do the same thing over and over again."

"That's where you're wrong. You could've used thick, heavy strokes and been done with this in two days, but your work is much more nuanced than that. See the richness in the red beginning to emerge?"

"Yeah, but it's only taken five years to get there," I say.

He laughs. "I think your leaves will see their peak in another week or so."

"After all the real leaves have fallen."

"True. But yours will last forever."

★

My nightmare is here. I don't know where to sit in the cafeteria. The band table is out of the question. Emma's using the camera on her phone to put on lip gloss, and Graham's leaning into the frame to check his hair. Emma rests her head on his shoulder so they can share the screen.

Maybe it *is* love. I should just go eat in the bathroom before they see me standing here. Before Emma sees me holding my tray all by myself. How could she *do* this? Two weeks ago, everything was fine, and now I don't even have anyone to eat lunch with. I don't know what to do. I don't know where to go.

I glance from table to table, with no luck. The same kids I've seen thousands of times are here, even the ones who nod at me in the hallway, but I don't know them. Not really. And they don't know me.

I whirl around to leave and almost knock over Abby in the process.

She jumps back, barely missing a collision with my tray.

"Sorry!" I blurt.

"Hey! I didn't know you had this lunch." Abby smiles, and I am so relieved to see her.

"Yeah, I don't usually stick around here long."

She nods slowly. "Same. You want to come with me? I was just grabbing a fork."

"You mean a spork?" I make a face and hold mine up where she can see the tiny prongs on the end.

"What, there are no forks now?" Confusion clouds her face. "Since when?"

"Since the book banning started and they became deadly weapons." I thought it was bad when the plastic prongs couldn't even puncture the cafeteria mystery meat. But in true Dogwood fashion, they made it worse in the name of safety. Now we have sporks, which break off in anything thicker than soup.

Abby rolls her eyes. "When will it end?"

We snag an extra spork and stroll past the whispers at the band table and out the door. The sensation of dozens of pairs of eyes following me ends the minute it swings shut. Tension drains from my shoulders. It's going to be okay.

"Rough day?"

She knows. How could she not? The whole school knows.

"I've had better." I shrug.

"That bad, huh?"

"It's half over. That's an improvement."

She pauses. "The improvement happened yesterday, if the rumors are true."

I smirk. "They are." How pathetic am I that other people see it as an immediate improvement, and it took me until yesterday to do something about it.

We round the corner and, to my surprise, head straight toward the library. I hesitate. Don't we need permission to take food into the library? Abby steps ahead of me through the door. "Hey, guys, look who I found."

Dan Fuller is halfway through a burger. The high five in the lobby makes more sense now. "Hey!"

Matt pauses with his peanut butter and jelly sandwich in midair. "It's about time, Ms. Harper!"

I smile back at him. Is this what it feels like to be popular?

"Hey," I say. I take a second to look around. The shelves are still as empty as before. "Really? You eat here?"

"Just since they emptied it." Dan smiles, his grin vibrant against his black skin. "But we're not supposed to."

"What?" I look over my shoulder at the door. "Aren't you worried about getting into trouble?"

He shrugs. "Nope. If they kick us out of here, we can go to the cafeteria or eat outside."

"And what about the substitute? What's her name—Ms. Morgan?" I whisper as I slide into a seat at the table.

"On the phone with her mother in the back during her lunch break. Every. Single. Day. She doesn't care if we eat in here." He takes a huge bite of burger.

"And she pretty much ignores us." Abby digs her spork into some sort of rice and chicken combo. Judging from the aroma wafting up from the chicken, no way is that from the cafeteria. "By the way, your timing with Graham couldn't have been better. We've been tiptoeing around

136

him for the last two weeks. That guy was bound to turn up something sooner or later, pacing the halls wearing that SCAR button."

I prod the scoop of tuna on my tray and frown. "He figured out I'm still reading."

"Oh no!" Abby groans. "There goes our library."

"I don't think he knows about the locker, or he would've said something. We ended things and that's it." I say it as though it's no big deal.

"Whew! That's good, but aren't you afraid he'll say something?" Matt asks. "Just knowing you're reading means he could really mess things up."

"I asked him if he was going to rat me out."

Dan chuckles. "And what did he say?"

"He said he didn't care about me or my books."

"Ugh! He's so mean." Abby drizzles some pink-hued sauce over her rice. "But I'm not so sure he's going to keep quiet. I've lived behind the Whitmores since preschool. That's long enough to know what happens when Graham doesn't get his way."

I smile. "He cries to his mommy?"

"Maybe." Abby shrugs. "Or he spills everything he knows to anyone who will listen."

"True. Remember in fourth grade when he tattled to

Mr. O'Brien every time I chewed gum?" Dan asks. "All because I didn't have enough to share one day."

"That was because of Graham?" Matt says. "They made you scrape gum off desks for a week every time you got busted!"

"Tell me about it," Dan says.

Abby twists the top off her water. "Yeah. If he couldn't have any, no one could." Her expression is thoughtful. "No way is he letting this go."

I force myself to swallow a bite of tuna. "I don't know. He's already using Emma to try to hurt me. Maybe he won't say anything. He has everything he wants now." *Her.* I should've said *her.*

"But only because you told him no. Then she was his only option, so he took it," Abby says.

I almost grin. I did tell him no, and it felt amazing.

"What actually happened?" Matt asks. "Graham found out you were reading, you ended it, and now he's with your best friend, right? Did I miss anything?"

Almost. I smash my entree with the back of my spork. "I think the last part may have been first." I grimace at the truth, but if my whole life is going to be out there in the open, I might as well set them straight.

"Unbelievable!" Abby rolls her eyes. "Well, we knew he was a jerk."

Funny. It took me longer to figure it out.

"I'm sorry," Matt says, flushing a bit. He looks like he'd like to crawl under the table. "I didn't know."

"It's okay," I say, dismissing it with a wave of my spork. I don't care anymore. They shouldn't, either.

"No, it isn't. You deserved better," Matt says.

I laugh. "Define *better*."

He considers me a moment. "Something real."

Real. I'd like to see what that looks like.

"You really don't think Graham has a clue about the locker?" Abby asks.

"Nope. I think we're safe for now," I say. "But we have to be more careful."

Everyone nods in agreement.

★

The soggy carpet of matted leaves squelches under my boots on the way home.

I don't know what I was expecting, but today wasn't it. All I know for sure is that Graham and Emma deserve each other.

I wonder how much of this year has actually been real.

I was so awkward this summer at band camp. And then, next thing I knew, Graham was flirting with *me*, June Harper. Not that I was able to date. Not officially. But he liked me. I just wanted to hold on to him and that magical feeling I got whenever he touched my hand.

Except I couldn't be myself around him. I had to hide who I was so I could be some idea of who he wanted me to be.

How did I miss it?

The toe of my boot connects with an acorn. I take careful aim and kick it as hard as I can, but it doesn't go far. The leaves slow it down.

All I could see before was the world according to my parents.

To Graham.

I didn't stop to think about how *I* saw things. If I had, maybe it wouldn't have taken me so long to get here.

12

EDITS

"**H**oney! Come down here a sec!"

Mom probably wants me to play along with her while she watches *Jeopardy!* I stash *Holes* under my nightstand and report for duty in the living room. Dad props his feet up on the ottoman, a grin on his face. "Well, look who it is."

"We have something important to tell you." Mom reaches over and squeezes his hand.

My heart picks up its pace. Maybe there's news about Ms. Bradshaw. Or maybe they've done something else. I'm afraid to ask, but I can't stop myself. "What is it?"

Mom smiles. "We thought it was time we return some things to you."

Does that mean what I think it means? "My books?"

Dad nods toward two boxes stacked in the corner. "It took us forever to read them all, but we finally did it."

"They're all here?" I try to hide my excitement, but it's impossible. Is it weird to want to hug books? Too bad if it is. It's what I'm going to do as soon as I get upstairs with them.

"More or less."

I don't like the sound of that, but I don't want to make them change their minds. "Thanks."

I have to take an armload at a time. Ten of them, actually, since the boxes are too heavy to lug upstairs. Surrounded by my collection, I sift through the piles and try to organize them. *Old Yeller* is first. I know this book so well. Each and every moment that makes me cry is committed to memory. I really don't know why I still read it when I know how it ends.

One of the pages toward the end feels thicker than the others, so I flip to it. A white index card has been glued down over the existing page. Travis is supposed to pick up his shotgun here, but instead it reads *And then Old Yeller was cured of rabies and lived happily ever after.* That's it. The rest of the pages have been ripped from the spine.

My jaw drops. I reach for another book.

My old copy of *Diary of a Wimpy Kid* has card stock glued over the fart jokes.

Monster is still there, but half of it has been torn out or rewritten in twelve-point Times New Roman font. Always glued over existing pages. A feeling of dread creeps over me.

The same edits are in a few of my other books. Someone took great care to cut out tiny black rectangles and paste them over certain words. They seem to have forgotten I've *already* read everything.

I don't know if I'm more angry or defeated. I never dreamed they could be this over-the-top.

I search for a book they couldn't possibly have edited. *Anne of Green Gables*. It's a classic, and I know Mom loved it at my age. But even Anne isn't safe. Her tea party with the currant wine is missing, and there's an index card in its place with the words *Anne serves grape juice to Diana. They have a nice tea.* The story doesn't make any sense without that scene.

I snap the book shut. This is exactly why locker 319 exists.

★

The next morning before school, a sixth grader whispers, "Shh! Here he comes again!"

Mr. Beeler has done three drive-bys so far with his walkie-talkie. I guess we do look a bit suspicious. The whole hallway is jammed tight with students, but there's no public event. No fundraising table. No flowers for sale. All of a sudden, this hallway's real estate value is on the rise without an obvious reason. And right now, I'm standing in the thick of it with Colby.

Mr. Beeler scans the students as he passes, nodding and greeting random people. His gaze lingers on me a moment longer than everyone else and makes my pulse quicken. I'm a question that he hasn't quite answered. And thanks to my detention with the litter crew, he's keeping a close watch on me. Clearly, I didn't think that one through.

Thank goodness for Abby, who works with the efficiency of a cruise director. She's already instructing the kids behind us. "You guys need to mix it up a bit. Don't look like you're waiting, and *don't* stare at June. Act like you're just hanging out, or he'll be onto us . . . if he isn't already."

We exchange a meaningful glance. It's just a matter of time if we're not more careful.

One of the teachers pushes his way into the end of

the hallway and squares his shoulders against the wall. The new technology lab teacher, I think. He crosses his arms and scowls into the crowd. What can he possibly say? We're not late for class, and we look like we're on our best behavior.

Abby appears by my elbow next to Colby. "Hey, you okay?" she asks.

"No," I say. "I'm not."

Matt drops his backpack next to me. "What did I miss?"

"You know how my parents took my books?"

They all nod.

"I got them back last night."

"That's great!" Colby says.

I look at each of them slowly and say, "They EDITED them."

Abby grimaces. "What?"

"As in they tore out entire pages they didn't like, rewrote endings, you name it."

Matt shakes his head. "No way."

"Wow," Abby says.

"You've got to be kidding me," Colby adds. I start to feel better just knowing my friends are as shocked as I am.

"I wish I were. Just when I think they're done, they do something else. It's never going to stop!"

Abby pats my shoulder. "Then it's a *really* good thing you have another library, isn't it?"

I smile. "Definitely."

Mr. New Tech Teacher starts walking in our direction.

"Code red!" Abby whispers. She turns to chat with some sixth graders, and Colby bends down to tie his shoe.

"Hey, can we talk for a sec?" Matt asks.

"Now?"

Matt's face says it all. *It can't wait.*

"Okay," I say. I carefully angle the notebook into locker 319 and secure the lock.

Cued by my exit, the throngs of students in line begin to disperse. Eek. We need to tell everyone to be less obvious about filling the hallway or leaving depending on whether I'm there. New Tech Teacher's eyes lock on me.

Matt casts a casual glance over his shoulder after we round the corner. "This is getting too risky."

It's like he read my mind. "I know. It's a good thing they don't know what they're looking for."

"Yeah, but it's too close. Graham already knows you're reading banned books. It wouldn't take much for him to put two and two together. Or for a teacher or principal

146

to catch on. June, we have to leave the locker and figure out something else. It's the only way we'll be safe." He takes my hand and my stomach flutters. The heat rises to my cheeks just to spite me. It's like my subconscious wants him to know what I think about him, when I'm not totally sure myself yet.

"What do you suggest?" I try to keep my voice steady as he leads me down the hallway.

He looks up and down the corridor and then drops my hand and reaches for a door handle. "I'd rather show you."

We cross the threshold together. Once upon a time, this wing of the building was the elementary school. This area was the gym, but it's so small we don't really use it for anything except end-of-the-year pizza parties. We're definitely not supposed to be in here unattended.

"Matt! This is great. Do they usually leave it un-locked?"

The door clicks into place behind us. "Every morning this week."

I grin. "You don't say."

"So, if you knew some people who, oh, I don't know, wanted a quiet space to read, I think you just found it." Matt winks, and my cheeks feel even warmer.

He's right. It's the perfect hiding place. It's exactly what we need. "Brilliant. Let's tell everyone about it at lunch."

He smiles. "Hey, I wanted to give you something, but it's not for your library, okay? It's something just for you." He steps closer.

"For me?" My voice comes out as a whisper.

He digs in his bag and hands me a flat brown package.

"Can I open it now?" I bite my bottom lip just the teensiest bit.

He shifts his weight to the other foot before he looks up at me. "Yeah." He smiles a crooked grin.

I'm not someone who opens things carefully to save paper. I rip right into it and am left holding *The Velveteen Rabbit* in my hands. The corners are bent, and the finish is smooth from years of use.

I have no idea what to say. "It's perfect." I don't know what I was expecting. But this gift actually screams *June Harper.*

He offers a shy smile. "I thought you could use a book your parents won't confiscate. Or edit. You can read this out in the open and everything."

I trace the outline of the rabbit on the cover with my finger. The finish there is extra thin, as though tiny fingers have also traced the bunny over time. "Thank you. I don't think they'll take this one."

He shakes his head. "They'd better not rewrite it, either! It's a classic."

I laugh. "That reminds me—did you know Old Yeller didn't die?"

The corners of his mouth twitch. "It's a miracle!" He whispers, "June, I think you're sitting on a gold mine."

"Shut up."

"It's true. You have the only copy in existence with a happy ending. You could probably retire off that."

I raise an eyebrow. "I'm so lucky." A strand of hair falls into my eyes.

"And I'm—" He lifts his hand to my face. Do it. Tuck my hair behind my ear. Oh my gosh, what is even happening? Breathe, June. Breathe.

But he stops himself and drops his hand. "I'm so late. See you at lunch?"

I tuck my own hair behind my ear and nod.

"Okay. Wait a minute after I leave so no one notices." He cracks the door and peeks out. "Catch you later, Supergirl."

I wave him on.

The Velveteen Rabbit. I lean against the wall and open the cover. Matt's name is written on the inside flap in large, childlike block letters. To the right, there's a note scribbled on the title page:

June,
    You deserve something Real because you ARE Real. You just don't know it yet.
    –Matt

Real. There's that word again. Not beautiful, not funny, not smart. Just *Real.*

A yellow Post-it note peeks out on a page toward the end. I flip to it and find an arrow pointing to this passage:

"You become. It takes a long time. That's why it doesn't happen often to people who break easily, or have sharp edges, or who have to be carefully kept. Generally, by the time you are Real, most of your hair has been loved off, and your eyes drop out and you get loose in the joints and very shabby. But these things don't matter at all, because once you are Real you can't be ugly, except to people who don't understand."

I slide down to the dusty hardwood floor with the book in my hands, staring at the words. Those beautiful words I know by heart that make me cry each time I read them, even though I can't tell you why. They look different to me somehow. Because they were Matt's. Because he wanted me to have them.

★

For the rest of the morning, it looks like the school is preparing for battle with all the teachers stationed in my hallway. During every class change, they study the crowd with coffee tumblers in hand. There are so many people in this corridor, I can hardly get to my lockers.

"Hey, hold up!" Abby jostles a few sixth graders out of the way and falls into step next to me. "I think we need to cool it for today."

I chuckle. "Whatever gave you that idea?"

She raises an eyebrow over her perfectly shaded eye makeup. "Yeah, well." She gestures to the crowd and I can't help but be jealous of her flawless black nail polish. I can't wear nail polish without it chipping off five minutes later. I blame my flute.

We both give silent messages to the kids around us. I give what I hope is an imperceptible shake of my head to

Olivia while Abby silently encourages a cluster of eighth graders to keep walking.

"It's time for us to go somewhere else," she says. "Like, tomorrow."

"I know. We should've moved locations the minute Graham and I broke up. I thought we were being careful, but"—I glance around us—"all he needs is this locker, and it's over."

Abby lowers her voice. "That's not going to happen, June. We'll be gone before anyone catches on!"

I grin at her. "I like the way you think."

The warning bell rings.

"Gotta go," Abby says. "See you at lunch!"

Twisting the lock's dial in semicircles, I tug down on the casing. It pops out of the joint and confirms to the surrounding authority figures that all is normal. I'm just a kid casually opening a locker with enough banned books to be expelled.

With my face blocking their view of my slightly ajar locker, I grin. Here I am in the open, and they don't even see me.

My fingers brush the side that houses my green spiral notebook. But instead of cardboard backing and looped wire, I touch cold metal. I dig deeper, but I'm still empty-handed. What if I've left it somewhere? No, that's silly. I know I put it back. I must not have put it in the right spot.

Taking a calming breath, I peek inside as much as I dare to open the door, and run my hand over every square inch of the locker as fast as I can. Then I lock it behind me. There's no point lingering where I can be caught.

The notebook is missing.

PROPERTY OF THE REBEL LIBRARIAN

Somewhere out there, someone has enough ammunition to bury me.

All it would take is for my notebook to fall into the wrong hands, and I'm finished at Dogwood Middle. Forget making it to thirteen. Forget high school. Forget finding out what Real means.

But I have to stay positive. There's a reason our names are nowhere in that notebook. All it says is *Property of the Rebel Librarian,* and that could be anyone. My stomach gurgles at the thought of someone connecting me to it. But there are no cameras anywhere near locker 319. They can't prove a thing.

Who could've taken it? And why? Do they hate banned

books? There are more than enough students in the Student Club for Appropriate Reading. If word got to them, they might do anything. A chill passes over me, popping goose bumps out all over my arms. Could this be something more personal? This is like one of those moments on a TV crime drama when the officers ask if you know anyone who'd want to hurt you.

I so do. Let me count the suspects:

1. Graham. He didn't know about my secret locker before, but what if he figured it out? He's still angry that I didn't choose him.
2. Emma. If Graham somehow found out, then she knows, too.

After that, I don't know. It could be anyone. But whoever it is, they've stood close enough to learn the combination for the lock. It wasn't broken, it wasn't damaged, and it opened just like it always does.

This means they know I'm using the locker. There's no anonymous librarian. They *know*.

The question is, what are they going to do about it?

By the time I get to lunch, I'm in panic mode. "But I just had it in my hands this morning."

Dan leans forward in his chair. "Are you sure you put it back?"

"Positive." I scrape a little matted gravy off the top of the tofu goo the cafeteria is calling beef tips. Dad got an email yesterday talking up the nutritional value of school lunches. So much for brown-bagging it. "I checked out *Rules* to a seventh grader, and then"—Matt told me we had to go, and then what? "I put it in locker 319."

"Time for us to move," Abby says.

I nod. "Past time."

"How about we set up in the gym tomorrow?" Matt says.

"The *gym*? Are you serious?" Abby says.

"He's talking about the old gym," I say. "It's been open this whole week."

Abby's curious gaze locks on me, and warmth creeps into my face.

Matt says, "I'm thinking we could have a lookout stationed outside the door just like we do in the hallway. Then inside, June could swap books out of her backpack." He smiles at me, and I feel his written words all over again. "That way we're not tied to the locker, and we're not creating traffic jams between classes."

"Yeah, but we'll be sitting ducks there," Abby says. "What if the person who stole the notebook knows it's us? What if it's Graham?"

"What if it's not?" Dan asks. "It could be some random person."

"Maybe it is, maybe it isn't." Matt balls up his napkin. "But either way, we can't go back to that locker."

★

"He's right. It's perfect," Abby says when I take her to the old gym.

"Yeah, I thought so, too." I spot the corner of a sketchbook sticking out of Abby's bag. "You draw?"

"Oh yeah."

"Can I see?" We sit on the bleachers together.

She nods and hands it to me. The first pencil drawing is a little boy on a swing that's so lifelike, I gasp. "Oh my gosh. This is amazing."

She looks down at her feet and smiles. "That's my brother. Carlos."

I turn the page again to find a small dog rolling over with a toy in its mouth.

"And who's this?"

"Sophie, the world's most rotten dog."

"She looks adorable."

Abby laughs. "She knows it, too."

I turn the page again and nearly drop the sketchbook. It's a cartoon of Mr. Beeler in his suit, standing with his fist raised to the sky. The dialogue bubble says *I MUST stop them from reading!* Behind him, there's a door that reads BATHROOM, and he has a book tucked under his other arm. The print is tiny, but I can still make out the title: *How to Ban Books.*

I laugh until I cry. "Abby Rodriguez! You are so *bad!*"

She grins. "I'm in good company."

"I had no idea you could draw like this. This is like really, really good."

"Thanks."

"I like art, too, but I'm more of a painter. My stuff is nothing like yours. Seriously, you could work for Pixar."

"You think?"

"Definitely. I'd love to see some of your other work. *Especially* if it's like this." I laugh at the drawing again.

She brightens. "You want to come over after school next week?"

"Yes!" It feels amazing to make plans with a friend, and suddenly I'm hit by how much I miss Emma.

"Do you have a sketchbook?" Abby asks.

I nod. "Yeah, but my pencil drawings are terrible. I'm better with watercolor."

"Oh stop. You should bring it with you. I want to see your stuff!"

"Maybe," I say. I've never shown any of my friends my work before outside art class.

No one's ever asked. I hand the sketchbook back to her, the cartoon of Mr. Beeler reminding me of locker 319. "So, who do you think took the notebook?"

"If it wasn't Graham, then I have no idea. But I don't think they'll keep us wondering long."

★

It's impossible to walk by the diner without salivating over the smell of fat from the deep fryer. Which is why when Matt asked if I wanted to go there after band, I didn't think twice about it. We're just friends heading to the diner, and there will be plenty of other kids there so it will be like a group thing.

The jingling bells clatter against the wooden door and announce our arrival to at least ten Dogwood Middle kids, and some from the high school. They're already wolfing down platters of onion rings and ice cream sundaes with extra whipped cream. I'd think I'd died and gone to heaven if half of them weren't wearing their SCAR buttons.

Pictures of varsity football players hang on the walls alongside pom-poms and a few framed jerseys from the 1950s. If it weren't for the high schoolers snapping pics with their phones at the booth in the corner, I'd think I'd stepped back in time. But I love it. It screams comfort and I'll take all I can get. It would only be more perfect if they had a band hat or two on display alongside all the sports.

Matt leads me to a booth with cracked red seats. To my left, barstools line the counter, and at the end, a jukebox plays tunes from decades ago. A senior I lent *Six of Crows* to during band yesterday waves from behind a menu. This thing is so big now, there are even high schoolers in on it.

Matt's brown eyes meet mine and I feel myself relax. There are people I've known my whole life that I've never really been comfortable around. And then there's Matt. We barely said two words to each other before this month, but when I'm around him, I don't get nervous at all.

He leans back and stretches his arm along the back of the seat. "I don't think I've ever seen you in here before."

"I've been grounded."

He cracks a smile. "The whole time you've been in middle school?"

I laugh. "Just lately. Before that, they didn't want me to eat too much junk food, and we only came here on special occasions."

"What can I get you to drink?" says a hard voice to my left.

I whip my head around so fast my ponytail swishes against my neck. Madison stands by our table looking ticked off. Of course. Her family owns the place. If I were ever allowed to come here, I might've known she helps out after school.

"I'll take a chocolate milk shake," Matt says.

She looks slightly flustered. A normal response when you're waiting on a cute guy who's sitting with someone you picked on all through elementary school.

"Cherry Coke, please." She's going to spit in it. I know it, just like I know a black widow spider will set up camp in our mailbox after the first tulips bloom this spring. It's what they do.

Her face stretches into a forced smile. It contrasts with the dark rings that rim her blue eyes. "I'll have that right out." And then she's gone.

"You know, when everything with the library started,

Madison told our whole class that she hated it anyway and didn't care. She doesn't like me, either."

"That's two strikes as far as I'm concerned." He winks.

I wish I could flirt back without looking like I'm in pain, but that's biologically impossible. So I just grin and shrug.

"Why does she hate you?"

I open my mouth to speak and then stop. "I don't—"

"One Cherry Coke and a chocolate shake." Madison places the drinks on the table and shifts her weight to one hip. "Know what you want yet?" She smirks. "Or should I get you a book while you think about it?"

Matt's jaw drops.

"What?" I say.

She dismisses me with a wave. "Oh, wait. I had that backward. You get *other* people books now, don't you?"

I shake my head while the color drains from my face and act like everything is fine. It isn't fine. Madison *knows*. "I'd like the special, with extra-crispy fries."

"Make that two."

She walks to the counter, impales the order on the metal spike, and spins the wheel back to the cook.

"I can't believe that just happened! June. She's not someone we want to know about us." Matt takes a sip of his milk shake. "What in the world happened with you two?"

"We were friends when we were little, but all that changed when Emma moved here." I shrug. "I started inviting Emma to play with us, and before I knew it, I was spending all my time with Emma. I didn't mean for it to happen. But it did, and Madison has hated me ever since."

He frowns. "What made Emma so great?"

In second grade, Emma moved here in the middle of the year and took the desk in front of mine. While she introduced herself at the front of the room, I spotted *Beezus and Ramona* and a Junie B. Jones book peeking out of her bag. I knew right then that we'd be friends. We bonded over books. And then there was so much more. Girl Scout camp, eavesdropping on Kate's phone calls, learning to play flute together. When her grandmother was really sick in the hospital, I brought Emma a book and she cried when she saw me. But I don't know how to say all of that. "We both loved books."

Matt shakes his head. "Really?"

"Yeah, well, I guess things changed. For everyone."

"And Madison is still upset about it. Is she upset enough to break into your locker?"

"I don't think so." I lean back in my seat. "You can't

say anything, okay? Right now you have"—I lean closer— "*maybe* a fifty-fifty chance of eating something without a loogie in it. I'd hate for you to up those odds." I grab his wrists. "Save yourself!"

He cracks up. I realize my hands are on his and release them as quickly as I found them. For just a second, I think about Emma. If she had seen that a few weeks ago, she would've been so upset. There's this unspoken rule that you're never supposed to like your best friend's crush. But I don't have a best friend anymore, and I don't think she even likes Matt. I don't owe her anything.

More students trickle in through the door. I'm glad we got here early. It's going to be standing room only soon.

Matt glances toward the kitchen. "I hate a bully."

"And I hate conflict."

He laughs. "You keep telling yourself that, rebel."

"I mean it." I really do. I think.

"Fine. You win. I won't say anything." He leans back against the seat, resigned. "But I'm worried she will."

"I think she wants to scare me more than anything. She likes to do that," I say.

"I don't like it."

"I know. Where were you when I was ten?"

"Working at my dad's garage, probably."

"Really?"

"Well, we can't all be Whitmores." He says *Whitmore* like it's something fancy. "Some of us have to work for what we have."

What do I say to that after crushing on Graham? What *can* I say? That I was wrong? That's an understatement. I really thought he liked me. I take a sip of Coke through my bendy straw.

This moment is slightly awkward. Or at least it feels that way to me. I don't know what to say, so I say nothing, and that somehow makes it worse. My ears perk up as the jukebox plays the first lines of a song I used to dance to in the backseat whenever it came on the car radio. "I love this song. Do you know it?"

"Know it?" He grins a wicked smile. "You have no idea."

I tilt my head slowly, but before I can say or do anything, he takes my hand and begins to sing in a gravelly voice.

A high schooler swivels on her barstool and grins. Most of my blood rises into my face as conversation halts around us. Two guys from my English class elbow each other from a few tables away. All I can hear is the sizzle of the grill, the melody of the jukebox, and Matt. Oh, and the hammering of my heart. There's no other sound.

"Stop!" I whisper. This isn't happening. Make it stop. Make it stop. Make it stop.

But he's not stopping.

He reaches his hand almost to my elbow, singing as loudly as he can. He twines his fingers with mine.

"Aww," the girl at the table behind us says.

He finishes the line and brings my hand to his heart. His heartbeat is solid. Steady. *Real.* My cheeks flush and I break into a huge smile. "You're making a scene!"

What's he even doing?

"Good," he says with a wink. He keeps singing.

I lose the next few lines. I'm mildly aware of everyone, including Madison, hovering to watch, but I'm lost in the golden flecks of his eyes and how they match the constellation of freckles on his cheeks.

The music builds to a crescendo. He leaps to his feet and belts out the next line with his head tipped back. He hits every note.

And then his voice softens and he brings it back down in full dramatic fashion. I feel his hand on mine again, and this time I give it a small squeeze. I can't help it. He squeezes my hand back and finishes the last line next to me.

The final note plays, and the entire place erupts in applause. Or maybe that's the sound of my heart exploding. Can't be sure.

He takes a bow, then gestures to me with his hand.

More applause. More *Aww*s. It's as though the restaurant has released a collective sigh of wistful longing. I don't even care if they're staring. I'm so happy, I could stay in this moment forever.

Matt chuckles.

I lean in close and say in a low voice, "You're in so much trouble."

He looks me right in the eyes. My heart is beating so fast I'm afraid he can hear it. "You're welcome," he says. There's something new in his face, but I can't pinpoint it. Mischief? No, that's always been there. It's more serious than that. Before I can figure it out, he slides back into his side of the booth, and I'm left with more questions than I started with.

What am I supposed to say? I need a moment to get myself together, so I look anywhere but at Matt. Like the front door, where Graham's hair gleams in the sunlight filtering through the glass. He and Emma stand by the cash register with their mouths gaping open.

Emma covers her mouth with her hand and whispers in his ear. He shrugs out of her grasp and rolls his eyes. Even from here, I can see a tiny pulse pinging in his cheek when his jaw clenches. Without a word, he tugs Emma's arm and they duck out the door.

Madison drops our plates in front of us with a clatter. There's no question of what else she can get us. No forced smile. She simply stares at me for a moment and then stalks back to the kitchen.

Matt leans over as if sharing a big secret and says matter-of-factly, "I don't think she liked my singing."

I laugh. "No, I don't think she did."

"Clearly, she has terrible taste."

I almost choke on a fry. I don't remember the last time I had this much fun, even if it means my parents will hear about it later. I don't care. They're going to know everything anyway. "I'm surprised you knew that song."

"Of course," he says, squeezing ketchup onto his cheeseburger. "My dad only listens to oldies in the garage, which means"—he points toward the jukebox—"I'm now taking requests for every song in there."

"I'm fine," I say quickly. One serenade was more than enough.

He chuckles. "Suit yourself."

I try to picture Matt as a fifth grader. He's standing on a stool because he's too short to reach, leaning over an engine and learning how to change the oil. Singing along to oldies. Wiping his small hands with a filthy rag. I want to hug the Matt in my mind, tell him what he's doing is valuable. Maybe I can't do that, but I can tell the real-life Matt sitting right in front of me. I don't care if I sound weird. I'm saying it. "I'm glad you work for what you have."

"I'd rather have a trust fund."

"I bet. But then it would be easy to take everything for granted."

"Nah. I'd appreciate all my lovely stuff. My new guitar, my new baritone, my new"—he rubs his chin—"what do you think? Porsche or Corvette?"

"You're thirteen. You can't drive."

He shrugs. "I'll have my learner's permit in two years."

I smile at the idea of Matt behind the wheel. What would it even be like to not have to walk everywhere after school? To ride with him?

"So, which one?"

"For you? Corvette. A convertible." But I think he'd be much happier if he found an older model and rebuilt it himself.

He nods with approval. "No way would I take that for granted."

"You say that now."

"You doubt?" He dips a fry into his milk shake and pops it into his mouth.

"I don't doubt *you*. But if you'd been born with all that, things would be different. You'd be different."

"Go on." He looks amused. "Different how?"

"The thing is, if you'd never worked for anything, you'd never really appreciate anything, either."

His eyes meet mine. "Or anyone," he says.

"Or anyone," I echo.

ACCUSATIONS

Just before dinner, Dad replaces the kitchen phone on the charger with more force than necessary. It snaps me out of replaying Matt's song in my head.

Mom looks up from her cutting board. "Honey? What is it?"

He swipes a cucumber slice from the tray and blurts out, "Kate changed her major."

The knife clatters out of Mom's hand. "What?"

I stop slicing cheese. Could it be? Did my rule-following sister stick a toe out of line? Please, spotlight, shine on Kate for a while.

"She wants to be a teacher." He looks genuinely panicked.

Mom wipes her hands on a dish towel. "A *teacher*? But she's *premed*." Her voice always gets screechy when she's anxious.

"*Was* premed." Dad clears a few pieces of cheese from my plate.

Mom looks as though she's just been told her expensive antiaging cream doesn't work.

"What does she want to teach?" I ask.

"*English*, of all things." He turns to me. "You'd better not get any bright ideas. We've worked too hard for you to just throw it all away."

"And those who can't do, teach. Everyone knows that," Mom adds.

My jaw drops. How can she say that when she spends so much time with my teachers? It seems like she'd think more of them than that.

She adds, "You've got too much potential for that sort of thing, June."

I shove a piece of cheese in my mouth so I won't smile. All this time, they've been hovering over me so much that they didn't see Kate's shift coming. No wonder we haven't heard from her.

"Wouldn't dream of it," I say. I dream of other things.

"Good. Because I've got news for you, young lady. You're going to medical school."

I don't have the perfect math and science grades for it, and even if I did, I don't like sick people. When I smell vomit, *I* vomit. I don't want to spend my life dry-heaving in a hospital. But that's a conversation for another day.

"We knew something was up when she didn't come home for fall break." Mom wipes her hands on the dish towel again.

Dad just stands there at the sink looking out the window. I don't think he sees what's actually there. He's seeing something else way beyond our yard.

Mom pats his shoulder.

"We'll get her straightened out at Thanksgiving," he says.

I pick up the block of cheese again and try to look indifferent. "What's so wrong with being a teacher?"

Dad sighs and hands me a tomato. "Keep slicing."

★

The next morning, I stroll to school, nursing my tumbler of hot chocolate. Its warmth insulates my hand from the chilly Halloween air. It's not quite cold enough for gloves yet, but it will be soon.

Matt reclines on the iron bench on Dogwood Middle's lawn. His arm is draped casually along the back of it, his head tilted toward the ground.

He opens his eyes as I approach. "About time, Harper."

"I didn't know I was late." I'm here earlier than usual.

His breath comes out in a puff of white in the cold. "What would you say if I told you we could rule out a suspect this morning?"

I'm not sure I like the sound of that. "I don't think—"

"Do you trust me?" I never noticed before how long his lashes are.

"Of course I trust you."

"That's all I needed to know." He leans forward. "I'm feeling festive, so we're breaking into Madison's locker."

"*We?* Oh no. Not happening. And who says she's a suspect, anyway?"

"She *knows* about the locker—or at least she knows about the books . . . and that we have a lot of them."

"So does half of the school! Are you going to break into other kids' lockers, too? How about Graham's?"

He tilts his head. "That's not a bad idea, but I think

we'd know by now if he'd figured it out and stolen the notebook."

"You're not doing this."

"Forget about Graham for a sec—with everything Madison said yesterday and what you told me about her . . . well, I just think we need to rule her out. It'll just take a minute, and then you'll know."

"No." I drop my backpack at his feet and sit next to him on the bench. "I won't do it. Checking her locker proves nothing. Even if she did it, who says it has to be in her locker? It could be in her bag or at her house." I wish I'd never told him about elementary school. Yes, Madison makes me nervous, but she could tell on me with or without the notebook. But what if she has it? "Leave her alone."

"Oh, look who it is," he says, nodding at the road.

"What?" I follow his gaze to Graham's mom's SUV whizzing around the corner to the drop-off circle. Graham steps out first, headphones on the back of his neck, followed by Emma. Of course, I realize a moment too late. Today is Graham's fourteenth birthday. His parents made good on their promise. He's wearing new headphones that cost more money than I've seen in my whole life.

Matt smirks. "I'll bet he breaks those headphones by lunchtime."

I giggle and elbow him in the ribs. "You're awful, Matt Brownlee."

"What?" he says with a grin. "He totally will. Now, are you going to help me or not?"

"No way. I want no part of this. Whoever took it will let us know soon enough."

He opens his mouth to speak and I hold out my hand to stop him. "*However*, if I were to be standing a little bit down the hall from you and saw someone coming, I might walk past you. Not that it would mean anything. Rules are important, you know."

"Oh," he says, his tone serious. "Believe me, I know." Am I really going to do this? It's not my best choice. I always follow the rules. Or at least the old June did, before locker 319. A smile plays on Matt's lips. He wants to help me. How can I not help him?

"I almost forgot." I fish in my bag below the Velcro enclosure and produce *Bob*. "Found it this morning."

"Thanks." He flips to the second page. " 'To Brendan—I'd wait forever just to see you again.' What a sap. Makes you wonder who this Brendan guy is."

"I'm more interested in who's writing the inscriptions. It's some heavy stuff."

Matt closes the book. "I always get the feeling I shouldn't be reading it, you know? Like I'm reading someone's private diary."

"But we're not. I mean, someone's been unloading them in the Little Free Library. They wouldn't do that if they didn't want us to see them." That's what I tell myself, anyway.

"Do you think maybe Brendan's mom gave them to him, and he died or something? And now she's giving them away in the neighborhood because she can't stand to look at them anymore?"

"Nah, I don't think that's it."

"Could be a brother and sister," Matt says.

"Ew, nope. Whoever is writing the messages is madly in love with Brendan."

"How can you tell?"

I can't say it without sounding cheesy. "I can feel the love in their words." And I want to know that kind of love. Someday.

He chuckles. "I think you just want a love story."

"No, it's more than that."

He looks amused. "Out with it, then."

I smile at him. "I don't know. They know this Brendan guy so well, and the messages are about love and missing him. It just feels like they've got a broken heart."

He sucks in his breath. "Well. Isn't that depressing."

"No. It's beautiful."

"How in the world is that beautiful?"

"They're sharing their books, words and all, so it wasn't wasted. It meant something."

"If you say so." He tucks the novel into his bag and extends his hand. "Moment of truth. Time to see what Madison has stashed."

After Matt's little scene in the diner, it might be harder than he thinks. We just gave everyone something to talk about. People were already staring at me because of the locker, but now, older girls I've never spoken to before go out of their way to smile at me and say hello, and guys clap Matt on the shoulder as he walks past. This isn't about me. It's about *us*. We are the buzzword of the day, even in circles beyond locker 319, and we're not even together. I don't think we are, anyway. I don't know what to think anymore.

"Is it just me," I say, "or is everyone staring?"

"It's not you. It's me." He waggles his eyebrows.

"Hilarious."

Just for fun, we walk by my locker in the now almost-deserted hallway. Mr. Beeler stands with his walkie-talkie clipped to his belt, scanning the lockers and poised for action. His expression is patient and alert, much like his face in his fishing pictures in his office. He has no idea the pond is dry.

"Her locker's in the science wing, right before the turn for the tech lab."

"Easy enough, we just need to figure out which one," Matt says. "Don't you have science first?"

"I do. She's in my class."

"Good. I'm just walking you there a few minutes early. If anyone asks." That's believable enough after yesterday's serenade.

"I don't know what you're talking about. You *are* just walking me to class."

Madison scowls up from her locker as we pass. Number 177. That wasn't so hard.

The next part is. I lean next to the classroom door, trying to be cool and casual.

Matt's eyes widen and he reaches out, catching my arm just in time. "Whoa. You okay?"

One more second, and I would've toppled over and

broken my face. Matt should've drafted someone else to do this. I'm completely hopeless.

"Fine," I say.

He holds me steady for a moment while I regain my balance. He smells so good. Like cinnamon gum and sporty body spray. Why can't we just forget the locker and stay out of trouble? That would be fine. He releases my hand and grins. "Have you ever noticed your ears turn pink when you're embarrassed?" And when I'm nervous or angry, but who's keeping track?

I cringe. I can't believe he actually said that. And now, just to make things worse, warmth floods into my ears with a vengeance. I'm going to die. "See you at lunch?"

"Yeah," he says.

Madison squeezes past us into the classroom with a dramatic eye roll. "Psst, I really think she hated your performance."

"Some people just don't appreciate good music," he says with a wink. "Wish me luck."

Why did I agree to this again? I don't do things like this. Ever. Matt glances up and down each hallway and then pulls something shiny out of his bag. It almost looks like small hedge clippers. I can't let him do this. It's *wrong*.

I take a step toward him, but I'm too late—he snips off the lock like it was an irritating hangnail and sends it clattering across the floor. No, no, no. This wasn't part of the deal. He slips the clippers back in his bag.

Matt lifts the lever and pulls the locker open. I kneel down to pretend-adjust my boot because there's nothing else for me to do. I'm the worst lookout of all time. Out of the corner of my eye, I see him rifle through the contents of her locker.

What if she didn't do it? I glance up at Matt, who gives a slight shake of his head. I knew he wouldn't find anything. And then my eyes catch something else.

A shiny black half-globe jutting from the ceiling.

A security camera.

And Matt is standing directly in front of it.

★

First period is the longest class of my entire life. The only thing I hear is when Ms. Langford says that heartbreak is called that for a reason. If you get your heart broken, it can actually stop beating for a moment. I wonder if that's what happened when I saw the camera in the hallway.

She drones on with the PowerPoint, but it's all I can do to act like I'm paying attention.

Madison glances at me, but I keep my eyes straight ahead. Does she know? If only I could get a lock on my nerves and stop my leg from shaking. All anyone has to do is look at me to know I'm a nervous wreck. Which I've been since the bell rang. It's just a matter of time until she finds the remains of her lock on the linoleum floor. Then they'll check the cameras. And they'll find Matt.

I knew it was a bad idea the moment he opened his mouth. Why did I say yes? Nothing about it even makes sense. *If* Madison stole it, she would never keep it in her locker. I think I'm in the clear with the camera, but what if—*what if*—I'm not?

And what if Matt gets in major trouble for it? They can't expel him for that, can they? I can't even imagine a Dogwood Middle without him in it, and I don't want to. He's the one person who really seems to get me. I drum my fingers on my desk. The suspense is killing—

The bell rings. Finally. I stride straight out the door and walk past Madison's locker without giving it a second glance. I duck into the old gym to search for Matt. Instead, I find a group of students reading with flashlights. I'm glad they listened when I said no overhead lights. I shake my head at the eighth grader who keeps requesting *Twilight* and tell her to check back tomorrow. I wish we had the whole series, but I haven't spotted a single one yet. I dart into the art room.

I gather my painting, brush, palette, and a few tubes of paint. I fill a mason jar halfway with water, then slide into my usual seat at the table. Everyone else does the same.

Emma strolls in and stares at me as she gathers her materials. I try to stay calm. But *what if* she knows something? Did she steal the notebook? Would she tell?

I try not to look at her while I repeat exactly what I did yesterday, and the day before that, and the day before that. The red has turned from pale hints of color to a deeper hue. Looking at it now, I can't believe the difference. Even though it took forever, each day made it into something bigger.

Emma threw out the banana portrait last week. Now she bites her lip in concentration while focusing on a bowl of pinecones in front of her.

The same day she trashed her work, Mr. Garcia told me I could maybe get special permission to take high school art next year. I'd love it, but I'm not sure if my parents would go for it. They'd probably want me to take some kind of health science class instead.

Emma steals a glance at me. I pretend I don't notice.

Or care. But I can't stop worrying about Matt. The note-book. Everything.

Mr. Garcia weaves through the tables back to us. He lingers over my shoulder. "Talk to me about what you're doing today, Ms. Harper."

Easy. The same thing I've done every day before now. "Adding more layers."

He shifts slightly. "I think it's a little bit more than that. See what you're doing around the edges of the leaves? And the veins inside them? The color is thicker there, but delicate. See the space around it?"

"I'm not sure what I'm doing there."

"Don't you see it? That's where you let in the light."

"NOTHING GOLD CAN STAY"

I'm so nervous, I skip the cafeteria and head straight for the library. For the first time ever, I beat everyone else there. I even beat Ms. Morgan's daily phone call. She sits at her computer desk next to a plastic jack-o'-lantern full of candy.

"Can I help you, dear?"

"I'm just waiting for some friends," I say.

"What?" Her pocket begins to buzz. "Excuse me." She disappears around the corner and shuts the door behind her. Just like clockwork.

I swipe some candy from her desk and slide into a chair at our usual table. It's not long before Abby arrives with her Star Wars lunch bag and chocolate milk. "Happy Halloween!" she says in a Count Dracula voice. Her smile fades. "June? What's wrong?"

Before I can answer, Matt strolls in through the door with a tray in his hand and his bag slung over his shoulder.

I breathe a sigh. "Where have you been?"

He gives me a funny look. "Class?"

Abby slides into the seat next to me right as Dan walks through the door. "Will someone tell me what's going on?" she asks.

"It's nothing," Matt says.

"It's more than nothing. Matt decided to play private investigator to find the notebook."

"So? That's a good thing, right?" Abby asks.

"So it included breaking into Madison Greene's locker," I say, resting my face in my hands.

"You did what?" Dan says. He sets down his tray with a frown. "That's not cool."

Matt digs his spork into a mound of canned corn. "Desperate times. Someone else did the same to locker 319. How do you think they got the notebook to start with?"

"There are just a few problems with that." I tick them

off on my fingers. "One, they knew for sure we had it. Two, they didn't break anything. And three—"

"Wait—he broke something?" Dan asks.

"He cut off her lock!" I say. I still can't believe he did that.

"I had to." Matt shakes his head. "We had to check."

Dan and Abby frown. I'm glad I'm not the only one who thinks it was a bad move.

I sigh. "And three, they didn't have to stand under a security camera to do it."

Matt's eyes widen in surprise. "No!"

I nod. "I'm so sorry."

"But I looked up. There wasn't one there." He puts down his spork.

"The exit sign blocked it. I saw it from the other side ten seconds too late." How could we not check the ceiling? It's School of Deviance 101: ALWAYS. CHECK. FOR. CAMERAS.

He groans. "Well, it's done now." He pokes at watery, muted-green asparagus on his tray. "They won't check the cameras unless she reports it, and she won't. Trust me. She had nothing in there worth stealing."

Dan sets down his chocolate milk. "No, she wouldn't." He leans in and lowers his voice, even though there's no

187

one but us here. "My mom said the diner's in trouble. Madison has had to help out for the last two months because her family can't afford to pay anyone. Think about it." If she's as pleasant to everyone else as she is me, she's not faring well with tips, either.

Matt looks taken aback.

"You have to replace her lock," I say.

"Fine. I'll pick one up tomorrow." He pushes the rest of his food away. He frowns while he tears his napkin into long strips. "And we still don't have the notebook."

"It'll turn up."

"Yeah, but where? Until that notebook is found, we're all at risk."

"Not really. *Batman*."

He smiles. We thought of everything.

The door swings open, and Mr. Beeler marches in flanked by our two school security guards. My heart sinks. "Matt Brownlee," Mr. Beeler says.

It's not a question. It's an accusation. This is all my fault. If Matt hadn't been trying so hard to help, and if I'd just said no, this wouldn't be happening. Adrenaline courses through my veins. Did they see me? If they had, they'd say my name, too, right?

Matt turns around, his face expressionless. "Yeah?"

It's as though Mr. Beeler just asked him if he wanted ketchup with his meat loaf.

I can't help but admire how calm he is. My voice would've squeaked.

"We need you to come with us. Now." Mr. Beeler nods to the officers. "Get his bag," he says. But he's watching me instead of Matt.

★

Matt wasn't in band and he didn't show up when after-school practice ended. It's like he disappeared into the principal's office and never came out. I set out for home after I've lingered as long as I can.

A few jack-o'-lanterns peek out from the shop windows, and a paper skeleton waves in the doorway of the diner. Threatening clouds darken the sky.

I hurry past it, remembering the music and how happy I was. I'm struck by the difference a day makes. Yesterday changed things between Matt and me, but he'll be grounded forever after today. I don't know what normally happens when kids do what Matt did, but they make you pick up litter now if you're caught reading books. So this will probably be ten times worse.

When I get to Maple Lane, the wind gusts and sends

fallen leaves into a dance around my feet. The branches are entirely bare now.

Today in the Little Free Library I find *Sticks & Stones* and *Poppy Mayberry, The Monday.* My copy of *The Graveyard Book* is back on the shelf.

I flip over to the message in the first book: *To Brendan—If I could be a Wednesday, I'd turn back time.* The writing inside *Sticks & Stones* says, *To Brendan—who's always known the power of words.* I've found my reading for tonight.

Stooping down, I slip the books into the hidden compartment in my backpack. I feel bad taking my own book again, but I'll swap it with something else soon. A dark shadow passes over the blinds in the front window. Someone is standing there watching me. Again. They could be someone's mom. They could even be Ms. Bradshaw, for all I know. I smile at the thought, even though there's no way that's true. If Ms. Bradshaw owned that house, she'd be halfway down the driveway by now asking which book I planned to read first. She wouldn't be hiding behind her blinds. I pull myself up to my full height. I can feel them watching me still. Without thinking, I hold up my hand and wave.

Nothing moves for a moment. And then the shadow passes again. A section of the blinds presses flat up against the window. There's no question about it. It's a hand waving back at me.

The wind blows my hair in every direction except the one that would give me any chance of looking like a cover model. Thunder booms, and I pick up my pace. Ahead of me one ruby-red leaf rattles sideways from a branch a few yards away.

It's beautiful. It can't stay, but it clings for dear life anyway. I stop to take a picture of it with my mind.

Then another strong gust of wind rips through the branches, and the last leaf falls.

★

"Hello?" I say. "Mom?"

"In here."

I follow her voice to the kitchen, where she sits with my dad. Each one has an enormous bowl of ice cream in front of them.

I sling down my bag and reach for a bowl.

"Don't even think about it," Mom says. "You'll spoil your dinner."

I bite my tongue. Why don't they just have burgers on the grill and make me eat tofu? It's like they know I didn't eat lunch.

"So, when were you going to tell us about the diner?" Dad says through a large bite of ice cream.

There's no way I'm going to share with them—if there's even anything to share. I shrug and tell them the truth. "I don't know."

Mom says, "Next time you get serenaded in public, a heads-up would be nice. I had to hear it from the cashier at the grocery store, and believe me, she told me *all* about it. *Very* interesting."

"Okay."

Dad leans back in his chair. "So, you went on a date."

"No. It wasn't a date. It was just a snack after school. Promise."

"A snack with singing."

"I didn't sing."

Mom puts down her spoon. "Your father and I were just wondering what kind of young man would choose such a romantic gesture." She pats the chair next to her. "We know nothing about him. You can tell me, or I'll just call his parents and find out for myself."

I can tell her or suffer eternal humiliation. Both probably end in being grounded again. I sigh. "Gee, when you
put it like that, how can I refuse?"

She raises an eyebrow. "Spill, kid."

I slink back into the uncomfortable wooden chair.
The rungs cut neat rows into my back. "Matt Brownlee is
in eighth grade. He plays baritone in the band—"

"And he sings," Mom adds.

"Yeah, that, too. His dad has a car shop. That's all I
know. You already met him, Mom. Remember?" And he
likes to read, but I think I'll leave out that part if I ever
want to see him again.

"When?"

"In the band room after your meeting. It was raining."

She leans back in her chair. "Oh, that's him?" She
nods. "I remember."

Dad props himself up on his elbows. "But you still
can't date him."

"Didn't even want to," I say. Why push my luck?

They exchange glances. I've never been good at lying.
And after the stunt Matt pulled today, it's only a matter
of time until my parents hear about it and I'm never allowed to hang out with him again.

"Well, good," Mom says. "Then it's settled. No dating."

"Sounds like a plan." Dad scrapes the last bit of ice cream out of the bowl. "When you're sixteen, we'll talk. Until then, no more diner trips alone. Or you're grounded." He flashes me his best smile.

COMPARTMENTS

The last thing I want to see when it's pouring rain and freezing is a line of students waiting to get into the building. I fall into place behind Brooke. "Is there a reason we're standing out here?"

"Some kind of random search," she says.

"Oh," I say, my voice slightly higher than usual. It was just a matter of time before they started searching for books. And me. But the secret compartment is there for a reason. They won't find anything unless they're looking at the stitches under a magnifying glass. But what about everyone else? I fidget with the strap on my backpack. "Must be important."

Brooke edges under my umbrella. "It's probably about books."

I grip my backpack strap tighter. "Yeah, I heard books have been a big problem lately."

The line inches forward just a bit.

I can't see a thing from outside. All I can do is roll my shoulders forward and take comforting sips of hot chocolate.

There's no sign of Matt anywhere, and still the line grows.

Brooke frantically tries to flatten her hair into place, but she's no match for sideways rain. "Speaking of which, what's going on with Matt?"

My stomach drops. "What do you mean?" I say, trying to sound as casual as possible.

"I was hoping you'd tell me, since I heard *all* about the diner." She sighs. "I didn't want to be the bearer of bad news, but you need to know this, okay? They're saying he stole a wad of money from Madison Greene's locker."

"No way! He wouldn't do that." I hope he's okay. This is all my fault. I never should've gone along with it.

Brooke shrugs. "I know. It doesn't sound like him at all. I'm just telling you what I heard. And that's not even the worst part." She leans back and speaks quietly. "They found a banned book in his bag."

Of course. I had just given him *Bob*. I suck in my breath like it's the most scandalous thing I've heard in months. "What?"

"You should've heard Emma. She's telling everyone she knew he was trouble and that's why she liked Graham instead."

"I guess she forgot to tell me." I don't even try to keep the sadness out of my voice.

The line moves forward a few feet more. Closer to a possible phone call to my parents. They're watching to see who leaves. If I step away, they'll catch up to me in less than a minute.

Brooke's hand flies to her mouth. "Oh, June! I'm sorry. I wasn't even thinking. If it makes you feel any better, she's driving me up the wall with her bragging. We're all sick of it. Oh, but I'm going to need to know more about the diner! Out with it." She leans in to whisper into my ear, covering her mouth with her hand so no one else can hear. "How long have you guys really been together?"

"Brooke!"

The line moves forward again. Stay calm. There's the

tiniest chance that I'll make it through the line without getting caught, but it isn't looking good.

She cackles. "Please say weeks. You don't know how much I'd love to tell Emma just to see her face."

"You know I wouldn't have done that to her."

Brooke's expression darkens. "Yeah, but *she* would've. Trust me, she's not the same."

I shrug. "I don't think anything is anymore. So when will Matt be back?"

"Don't know. He's suspended until they finish their investigation."

I really should talk to Brooke more often, even if she won't share her junk food. She's like a walking student gossip columnist.

Two sixth graders in front of us disappear into the building. In just a moment, we'll be out of the rain, and I'll find out if I'm going to live another day without breaking my parents' hearts. I hope.

Brooke's eyes widen. "Oh my gosh! Do your parents know about Matt?"

"Oh yeah. My parents know everything around here." If they don't know yet, they will soon. Wait. They should've known about today's search. Why didn't they say anything about it?

"Oh. Okay." She looks slightly disappointed. The doors open, and Brooke and I step inside. The rain drips from our clothing and umbrellas and adds to the substantial puddle spilling from the waterlogged welcome mats.

The line leads to a table staffed by two security officers. We step up to the empty slot ahead. "Bags down first, ladies," one officer says, gesturing to the card table in front of him. They have to have found books on other kids by now. That means they'll be looking extra hard. "One at a time."

Brooke's bag goes first while I stand there helpless, watching my bag move up in the queue. I can't move. I can't breathe. I picture the look on Dad's face when they show him my bag. The betrayal he'll feel. Mom's panic when I get a lot worse than detention.

The officer runs his purple-gloved hand down the sides of my bag. But instead of placing his other hand on the opposite side to feel for gaps, he holds up the strap so he can shine his flashlight into the bag. Don't see it. Don't see it. I'm staring so intently at him that I don't hear the other officer call for me to move forward. "Today, please," he says.

I do as he says.

The officer finishes with my bag and pushes it to the

end of the table. I'm just zipping it shut when a whizzing movement, like something being tossed through the air, catches my eye over the standing crowd. I follow it to the ground.

I wish I hadn't.

A trash bin from the cafeteria overflows with novels. My novels. Mr. Beeler stands with his arms crossed, his eyes growing bigger with each book added to the pile.

They found what they were looking for.

FAULT LINE

Abby pulls the gym door shut behind me, looking genuinely worried. "You're sure no one followed you?"

"Positive. They're too busy working the front doors. You could roller-skate down the hall right now and no one would say anything." I squint at her in the dim light. "No flashlight?"

"I don't feel like being expelled."

"You can't get expelled for standing in a gym. We'd get our hands slapped, tops."

Even in the shadows, I can see the irritation lining her features. "Um, have you met these people? I wouldn't put it past them right now. They could expel us for the other stuff we've done."

"They'd have to prove it. Do you have anything with you?"

"In my locker, but it's only there because I had to babysit last night. If it had been any other morning, June, I'd be sitting in Mr. Beeler's office now. You?"

I pat the bottom of my book bag.

She laughs. "I should've known." She slouches against the wall. "Hardly seems fair, does it? We're still getting away with it while everyone else gets busted."

"I know. I feel terrible."

"Right?" She sighs. "But they knew the risks."

"We all did. Rule number one: Don't get caught."

We sit on the cold floor.

"What are we going to do?" I ask.

Abby shakes her head. "There's nothing we *can* do. We can't help them. We can't get the books back. It's over."

"Not yet, it isn't. Mr. Beeler doesn't know about the locker. And not everyone got caught, you know."

She chuckles. "Did you *see* Mr. Beeler's face? Priceless."

"Right? They just kept piling up. I think half the school is in his office right now."

"As long as they remember rule number two," I say.

"Yeah. They'd better."

Don't squeal.

★

All anyone wants to talk about is who got busted this morning. I don't blame them. Not when at least three students from my science class are missing. Near the end of the period, Ms. Langford says, "Remember, it's so important that you know this so you'll do well on the state exam. It's fifteen percent of your grade, so if I were you, I'd pay *very* close attention to—"

The intercom crackles to life. Mr. Beeler's voice barks, "Students, faculty, and staff, it is a dark day here at Dogwood Middle. We need your help."

Ms. Langford resigns herself to listening at her desk.

Mr. Beeler clears his threat. "If you know of anyone in possession of banned books, please notify a staff member immediately. Remember, any student caught with illegal books will face severe consequences. There will be an emergency PTSA meeting immediately following sixth period today to address this issue. I hope you'll all plan to attend."

My mouth goes dry. Since when do they want us to go to PTSA meetings? I try to stay calm, but it gets harder with every passing second. First, my parents had to have known about the search today, and they didn't tell me. And now they're coming here? They can't know I'm involved, can they?

The intercom hisses, and then Mr. Beeler says, "One more thing: any student providing accurate information will receive a free yearbook this year." There's a final crackle, and then silence.

I keep my eyes locked on the whiteboard, but it doesn't matter. The whole room stares at me.

Whatever I thought I could get away with—whatever I dreamed I could build right under their noses—the game has changed.

LOST AND FOUND

Mom barges into the band room as soon as class ends and makes a beeline toward my seat. "Well? Where's this Matt?"

I take a step back. "I haven't seen him today," I say in a low voice.

She glances at the corner where Graham and Emma are hugging. Her features pinch together like she's just seen something horrific. "We need to address public displays of affection in the schools. That's next."

The loudspeaker blasts in the cavernous space and rattles against the walls. "Students, parents, teachers, and staff, the auditorium is now open. Please begin making your way there for this afternoon's meeting. We will begin promptly at three-forty-five."

"Well, I guess we'd better head that way," Mom says.

There's already a line outside the auditorium, and people continue to stream in from the parking lot. Mom probably led the charge on the phone tree to notify all the parents. I can't believe how many students are here. There are usually a few like me who are forced to come on occasion, but this isn't normal. They can't all be part of SCAR. We take our place in line behind Ms. Gibson.

I've stood in two lines too many today.

"I guess you heard about this morning," I say.

"Heard about it? Ha! My phone's been ringing off the hook. We're all shell-shocked. I'm just glad it's not you."

My throat feels like it has sawdust in it all over again.

"Your father and I both are. Can you imagine how all those parents felt when they received phone calls today? They must be so mortified."

I shouldn't say anything, but I can't help myself. "It's not like the parents did it."

She turns away from the growing crowd and looks me in the eye. "Like it or not, what children do reflects on their parents." She wraps her arm around me and squeezes my shoulder. "Which is why we've never been so proud."

And I've never felt so guilty. I don't deserve any of the nice things she's saying. "I'm nothing special," I say. My boots are so interesting right now, I keep my eyes fixed on them.

"I mean it, June. You really stepped up this month. I know it wasn't easy, but we wouldn't have done it if it hadn't been for your own good. Trust me, you'll understand someday when you have your own kids."

Even if I live long enough to have kids *and* grandkids, I don't think I'll ever under—

The loudspeaker roars back to life. "Attention. Attention, please. If you are not staying for the meeting, you should exit the building immediately. Please report directly to the auditorium if you wish to attend the PTSA meeting."

The crowd surges forward, and we move with it.

I want to crawl into a hole and stay there until summer. No, scratch that. High school. Unfortunately, that's not an option.

"Just think of it. We're here at this meeting today to fix a school-wide problem, and you get to hold your head up high knowing you rose above it all. That has to feel pretty good."

"Fantastic," I say. My voice betrays me with a flat monotone instead of the chipper response I was going for.

We pass through the double doors.

"Can we sit in the back?" I whisper.

"Nope. I'm going to show you off." She strides all the way to the very front, and I trail after her, silently wishing I had an invisibility cloak. Madison's eyes follow me down the aisle. Guess she gave up a shift at the diner to witness my downfall. Or worse, to signal it.

Off to each side of the stage, burgundy curtains are tied back with coils of golden ropes. Across the table in the center is a dark cloth topped with water glasses and a pitcher beading at the sides with condensation. The leaders of the PTSA sit at the table talking quietly among themselves, with Dad and Mrs. Whitmore to the right. Dad's face brightens when he sees me. Mrs. Whitmore's does not.

Mr. Beeler is off to the side, novel in hand, locked in an intense conversation with a dark-haired reporter. A small camera crew stands in front of them, the little red light on their camera aglow.

I slouch down in my seat. Eyes follow my every movement. I won't react because I can keep a secret, even when my insides are churning. But can everyone else?

The double doors creak to a close behind us, and the house lights flicker. Mr. Beeler taps the mic, sending a screech through the speakers.

I cringe.

"Good afternoon," Mr. Beeler says. "We have called this emergency meeting to address a problem at Dogwood Middle. As many of you have heard, we collected two hundred forty-two novels from the student body this morning." A collective gasp ripples through the audience. He takes off his glasses and rubs the bridge of his nose. "This isn't an isolated case of one or two books. It is far worse than that. This is a—a movement that has gripped our students." He replaces his glasses and shouts into the mic. "And I want it stopped!"

Mom nods.

"Parents, you may have noticed your children withdrawing over the last few weeks. Are they spending more time in their bedrooms? Do they arrive at school early and stay late? We've all noticed an increase in hallway traffic in key areas of the building. Given the number of books discovered this morning, we have our answer. Which is why all lockers are being searched by the safety committee at this very moment."

I breathe in. I breathe out. I am the picture of serenity. My mother pats my hand as if to say, *See why we were so hard on you?*

I try to picture locker 319 in my mind. The neat rows of novels stacked by genre in alphabetical order. They'll have a field day with it, except for one thing: no one has any ties at all to the locker.

Not even me. I cover my smile with my hand and fake a yawn. Even if the notebook turns up, so what? Our names aren't in it.

Mr. Beeler nods at someone offstage.

A blue bin rolls under the spotlights, flanked by two eighth graders. The wheels squeak under the weight of the contents. Something deep inside me cracks.

When it reaches the center area in front of the table, the guys tip over the bin. Books rush out in a mound. The auditorium is deathly silent except for the sound of rustling papers. So many books. I haven't seen them all in one place since this whole thing started. It's beautiful. And my heart is breaking because it's just a matter of time before they find the rest of them.

The guys give the bin a final heave, knocking out the books jammed at the bottom.

Mr. Beeler rises from the table. "That's all, boys. Thank you." They disappear into the shadows. Mr. Beeler plucks a book from the pile. "I had no idea what was really happening in my school." He holds the book up to the audience. *"Doll Bones."* He grimaces. "What *are* these kids reading?" I glance over my shoulder, only to find an entire auditorium of parents nodding in agreement. There isn't one reasonable adult in the whole place? I rest my chin on my hand and resign myself to watching. Mr. Beeler tosses the book down and snatches another. *"The Lightning Thief."* He casts it onto the pile.

I can't help but think of Matt. What did he say about that one? He loved the Greek mythology and said it was funny.

Mr. Beeler nudges the pile with his foot. *"Harry Potter and the Sorcerer's Stone.* Witchcraft." His face contorts in distaste. "I expect better. I *demand* better."

Better than Harry Potter? Good luck with that.

Mom gives a vigorous nod.

Dad looks right at me and smiles. The skin around his eyes crinkles, which means he's genuinely happy. I shrink down in my seat.

The back door opens. Mr. Hawkins walks in with a loaded library cart and says the three words I most dread: "We found it." There's my library for all to see. My life's work.

The murmurs are deafening.

An eternity passes with each step Mr. Hawkins takes toward the stage. People crane their necks toward me.

Mr. Beeler crouches down while Mr. Hawkins whispers in hushed tones. Mr. Beeler nods, then stands to address everyone. "Ladies and gentlemen, it appears we have our answer." He gestures to the rolling cart parked in front of the stage. "Locker 319."

Not one student makes a sound.

"Locker space at this school, used to house illegal literature." He mops his forehead with a handkerchief and stuffs it in his pocket. "Parents, I know you want answers. Unfortunately, there is no registered owner of this locker, which makes the offense even more serious."

More whispers from the crowd.

"Some of you—no, many of you—know the identity of the person responsible for this. I would urge you now to come forward."

The hum of the heater rests on my ears. A single bead of sweat trickles down my neck.

No one speaks. No one moves. With each passing

moment, I grow more hopeful. Is it even possible that out of the whole student body, no one is going to squeal? Not even Graham or Emma? I've never felt more accepted than I do right now.

Mr. Beeler stares at each quadrant of the audience. This is that thing teachers do when they want to see who looks away. Then they stare at everyone else until they spill what they know. When his gaze falls upon my row, I stare back at him without flinching.

Each second stretches into forever while the air grows more and more stifling. Every nerve in my body is set to go off from sheer panic. I will not fidget. I'm innocent until proven guilty.

"Folks, I guess that's it for now. We'll keep all of you posted if there are new developments. Have a good evening."

Mr. Hawkins darts through the side door ahead of the crowd, and the news crew follows behind him. I force myself to relax my shoulders. It's over.

"Wait!" A parent steps toward the stage, smiling broadly and waving a large manila envelope at Mr. Beeler.

The crowd stops.

"I just found this envelope under my seat. It's addressed to you—from a Graham Whitmore and . . ."

Heat creeps up my neck, straight to my ears.

"Emma Davenport."

My mouth falls open. I can't breathe. It's like my lungs are getting smaller by the second. Mom nudges me with her elbow, her forehead creased with worry.

Mr. Beeler perks up. "Oh?"

The parent hands the envelope to him.

Mr. Beeler tears into it and drops the shredded pieces on the floor by the mountain of books.

He holds a green notebook in his hands, examining a few pages at a time.

I'm going to be sick. All those times Graham stood next to my locker, he was memorizing my locker combination. How could I have been so clueless? And then he must have realized I didn't have a lock on my locker anymore. He didn't have to look very far to find it.

Mr. Beeler turns the pages faster. "Well. I had hoped for the name of the person responsible for this. Instead, I know the reading preferences of every superhero in this school."

A low murmur ripples through the crowd. He shakes his head. "I don't see one actual student name in this entire book. But I have dates. I have titles. And some of you, it seems, even have overdue books." He snaps the notebook shut and frowns. "It's one thing to run an il-legal library on public property. But to write this on the cover?" He holds up the notebook with my distinctive scrawl for all to see.

And there are those words I wrote just a few short weeks ago:

PROPERTY OF THE REBEL LIBRARIAN

Mom stiffens next to me. My handwriting.

My reaction is crucial. One misstep, and I might as well confess to the whole auditorium. I glance up at the notebook with my best bored expression.

There will be no confession tonight. Rule number one: Don't get caught.

And then Mom turns to me and speaks carefully mea-sured words that echo over the rickety wooden seats into infinity. "Alma June Harper. How could you?"

19

FALLOUT

Suspension sounds like it could be fun. You get to stay home from school. Watch TV, play video games, spend entirely too much time on your phone—if you have one.

Not in my family. After completing homework, my options are: practice my flute, fix dinner for the family, stare out the window, clean the baseboards (Dad's idea), or scrub the kitchen floor with a toothbrush. And that's just on Monday. I don't go back to school until Friday, so it's going to be a long week.

It's while I'm chopping cucumbers in the kitchen that Mom perches on the couch and flips on the local news. I hover at the edge of the counter to stay in sight of the television. The news anchor at the desk says, "In a freak lightning accident last night, residents of this tight-knit community were devastated when their beloved pecan statue was struck. The enormous nut toppled over and landed in a pasture. No cows were harmed. And now, we go to Dogwood Middle with Moira."

Immediately, I recognize the reporter with the dark curly hair. She was at the PTSA meeting on Friday. Now she wears a crisp blazer and stands in a familiar hallway of Dogwood Middle.

She smiles into the camera. "Hi, I'm Moira Roberts, and this is the news at six. Tensions are running high today in the halls of Dogwood Middle after a controversial PTSA meeting last week." We see books being dumped across the stage and silent footage of Mr. Beeler waving a book around. "Classic literature was confiscated on the basis that it was not morally sound for young people." The camera cuts back to her. "But they couldn't collect all of it. What school officials did not anticipate is that students would find a way to fight back."

I put down the knife.

The camera cuts back in a wide shot. "I'm standing in the Dogwood Middle lobby, where, as you can see, not everyone is in agreement with the limits put on student freedom." She points to specific messages on the wall.

The camera zooms in, and my jaw drops. The Student Club for Appropriate Reading propaganda is gone. In its place, pages from banned books paper every square inch of wall space. "Here we have *Matilda, Rules,* and *The Graveyard Book,* just to name a few. You'll also notice homemade signs with words like *freedom, choice,* and *listen.*" I spot a familiar cartoon of Mr. Beeler with his fist in the air and a book under his arm.

Is this really happening?

"Students have mixed feelings about the actions in their school," the newscaster says.

Abby's face appears on camera. Below her face, the text flashes, *Abby Rodriguez, Eighth Grade.* Abby says, "I think it's important to consider all points of view, which no one has done until now. This is a wake-up call. If I were Mr. Beeler, I'd pay attention."

"Ha!" Mom says from the couch.

"But not everyone thinks that," Moira Roberts continues. "Here with me is Graham Whitmore." His name and the subtitle *President of the Student Club for Appropriate Reading* appear at the lower left side of the screen. "How do you feel about this demonstration?"

"I think it's disgraceful." He looks right into the lens. "And cowardly. We've worked so hard to protect the students, and for someone to paper the walls with what we've removed—well, it just hurts."

I don't know how I ever liked him.

The camera is back on Moira Roberts. "School officials have no leads as to who's responsible for these postings, thanks to a malfunction of central security cameras over the weekend. But the protestors didn't stop with the lobby." The camera follows her across the corridor. "The pages continue throughout the building. Cleanup crews have been at it since this morning, but they've scarcely made a dent due to the heavy-duty adhesive." She stops in a familiar hallway. "This area seems to be the hub, with locker 319 as the focal point." The camera zooms in on the locker.

In neat red letters, LONG LIVE THE REBEL LIBRARIAN is painted across the glued-on pages.

Mom gasps from the couch.

"Wow," I whisper. The biggest smile of my life spreads across my face.

The camera zooms in on the reporter's face. "The message can't get any clearer than that, but will the school board listen? Find out tomorrow night when I report live at six. I'm Moira Roberts, and this is your Dogwood."

I have to hand it to whoever did it—they just scored legendary status.

★

By the time Dad emerges from his office that evening, I'm taking the garlic rolls out of the oven and setting Parmesan cheese on the table. "Something smells good," he says. Spaghetti is the only thing I can make without burning it.

The phone rings, but they both ignore it.

"It's ready when you guys are."

Mom flicks off the TV and wraps her arms around Dad. "Have you seen the news?"

"I wish I hadn't," he says.

At least they know I didn't do it. There are some benefits to house arrest after all.

The phone rings constantly throughout dinner. Finally, Dad gets up and takes it off the hook. "June," he says over dessert, "we need to go over what you're going to say tomorrow." The school board is holding an emergency session to deal with everything, and my parents have arranged for me to publicly apologize.

"What's there to talk about?"

Mom grimaces. "You need to tell the board how sorry you are."

I smush the brownie crumbs down in the bowl with my spoon. "I'm not sorry." There's no need to lie about it anymore.

Dad sighs. "But you should be. You *will* tell them it will never happen again, and that you'll have to live with what you did for the rest of your life." He takes a slow sip of coffee. "You do that, and maybe by this time next year, it will have blown over."

"I didn't commit a crime." I look from Dad to Mom. "I opened a library."

Mom touches Dad's arm. "What you did was *wrong,* and when you're wrong, you apologize." She shakes her head. "End of discussion."

LIGHTNING

No matter what I do, I can't calm my jumpy stomach and my sweating palms. I haven't had a single chance this whole time to speak up for myself. At least, not to anyone besides my parents, and they won't listen. But in eight hours, I get the floor for five whole minutes. They can't cut me off—I already checked. It's in the bylaws.

It's only ten o'clock, and so far Mom has put me to work dusting the blinds, spot-cleaning the couch, and changing the water filter in the fridge. At least it gives me something to do while I work through what I'm going to say.

The phone rings. "I'll get it!" I toss my sponge in the sink and run to grab it. "Hello?"

"*June!* You're home."

"Kate?" I'm so surprised and happy to hear her voice, I could cry.

"Turn on CNN. Right now!"

I rush for the remote and flip to the channel as quickly as I can. I sink into the love seat. "Oh no."

Kate and I are both silent while Moira Roberts's story replays. This time I see more footage from the meeting. The parents and students filing through the double doors. The guys dumping books onto the stage. Mr. Beeler at the podium.

The video stops on locker 319. This time the whole world can see how neatly someone painted LONG LIVE THE REBEL LIBRARIAN.

The camera zooms out, revealing the image on-screen behind the news anchor at her desk. "There's a developing controversy in the small town of Dogwood tonight. Just who is the Rebel Librarian? What provoked an entire community into censoring literature? Find out tonight, when we report live from Dogwood Middle."

Her co-anchor laughs and says, "Our crew had better be careful down there. Their script copy might get confiscated."

The anchor winks and says, "The school officials will have to pry it out of their hands first."

They cut to the weather.

"June, *what* is going on down there? I talked to some people I graduated with, and it's all anyone's talking about. They say"—she takes a deep breath—"they're saying you got this whole thing started."

"That would be something, wouldn't it?" It's like she's shocked I'm at the center of everything.

"Tell me it's true!"

I'd rather hear her grovel. "How could you just leave me alone here? With *them*? You haven't even called me back. You *knew* they took my books, and you dropped off the face of the planet. Do you have any idea what it's been like for me? I needed you." She should know. They used to watch her every move. Super-early curfew, no cell phone. And now they've only gotten worse.

There's a pause on the other end. "Look. I know, okay? I know they're strict—"

"They're ridiculous!" And so much more, but I don't have the words.

"I'm so sorry. Mom said you were grounded and couldn't talk!"

"Since *when* has that stopped you?"

"I know, I know. I just—I didn't want to call until I figured things out."

"Well, I'm so glad you took some time for yourself." Tears well in my eyes, and I blink them back.

"June, I—"

"Save it. You said you'd be just a phone call away, or did you forget that part?"

"I didn't forget."

I say nothing.

Kate takes a deep breath. "Things haven't been easy for me, either. I've been so alone. I had to make a decision that would decide my whole life, and I didn't have anyone to talk to about it. It's been awful trying to figure out what to do."

"I know the feeling."

She groans. "I just—June, I think about you all the time."

I almost smile. "Yeah?"

"Yeah."

"And what a jerk you are for ditching me?" She's not getting off the hook so easily.

There's a pause. "Especially that."

I think she means it. "Good."

"I'm sorry, June. Really. And whatever it is, I'm here now."

My shoulders relax against the couch cushions. "You

can't ever leave me like that again. All I had to entertain myself was your old diary, and it was so boring."

"You didn't!"

"I had nothing else to read," I say, totally serious.

"No! You wouldn't do that!"

I wait until I can picture her face turning red. "But Mom and Dad confiscated it, so I didn't get to finish. They read all of it, though."

"I'm going to be sick."

"Just kidding!" I laugh.

Kate sighs. "I guess I deserved that. So, what happened? Are you the news story?"

"Yeah." I feel so much lighter the minute the word leaves my lips.

"I knew it!" She laughs like I haven't heard her laugh in years, and the sound is infectious. I've missed her so much. "Look at my baby sister, all famous!"

"Not yet, anyway. Guess that's later tonight. You should thank me, you know. I'm making your career change seem like a new haircut."

She cackles. "How can I ever repay you?"

"I'm sure I'll think of something." Like letting me crash in your dorm room when I need space to breathe.

"So what happens now? Public outrage?"

I snicker. "That was Friday. But tonight's meeting should be a close second." I sprawl out across the cushions and drape my arm across my eyes. "I'll apologize and life will go back to normal." It sounds so simple like that. Maybe it is.

"Amazing. I'm hundreds of miles away and I still feel like I'm suffocating." She snorts. "I can hear Mom now." She switches to a superior tone. *"June, what were you thinking?"*

That's easy. "That I was the only one thinking."

"Well, someone needs to." She pauses. "And did you make other people think?"

"At least half the school." That counts for something.

She giggles. "Then that makes you the most dangerous person in Dogwood." With Kate on my side, I feel a lot more confident than I did a few minutes ago. It's enough to make me believe anything is possible tonight.

"I'm starting to figure that out. They don't like books, kids thinking for themselves, anything like that."

"Neither does that Whitmore kid. I'll bet he's superproud of that judgy interview. Someone said he was your boyfriend. It's not true, is it?"

"He's not my boyfriend."

"Ugh, it's like I live in a time vacuum. I don't know anything that's going on."

I clear my throat.

"Yeah, okay. That's my fault. But I *knew* you still weren't allowed to date!"

I laugh. And then I tell her everything. About Ms. Bradshaw, the canceled author event. How I got my hands on forbidden books. How I lost Graham and Emma but found Matt and Abby. How all of a sudden, people knew my name, and we were in something together much bigger than we dreamed it could be. I only skip the part about Matt at the diner. That's just for me.

"Anyway, Mom and Dad say I have to apologize to the school board. They told me it would build character."

"That sounds about right." She pauses. "You're not going to do it, are you?"

Even when she can't see my face, she can still read me. "I just—I want what I did to mean something."

"Oh, I think you've managed that, Ms. CNN."

"No, really. What good was any of it if nothing sticks? We still have no books. What about that? And what if I apologize and nothing ever changes?"

She sighs. "Listen to me. You have *one* shot at this.

Make them hear you. Don't waste it. And if Mom and Dad aren't happy when it's over, this conversation never happened."

I laugh. Maybe it's the pressure I'm feeling. Maybe I'm just on a roll and speaking my mind. Or maybe it's easier to say this without having to look her in the eye. I just know it needs to be said. "Hey, Kate?"

"Yeah?"

"I don't care what Dad says. You're going to be an incredible teacher."

There's silence on the other end. I wait a moment for her to speak. She doesn't. "Kate? You there?"

"Thanks," she says. Her voice cracks on the word.

"I wish you could be here tonight."

"Me too. I'll be watching. Make me proud."

I hang up the phone with a shiver. So many people will be watching.

★

I don't say anything on the way to the meeting. Instead, I lean my head against the window and brace for the storm in the auditorium.

Dad turns onto the school drive, and it looks like a celebrity has come to visit. News vehicles line the streets, the parking lot is full, and there are adults I don't even recognize streaming through the doors.

This is a big deal.

"Now, June, remember what we talked about."

"Got it, Mom." She only drilled me on my speech ten times before we left the house, but who's counting?

Dad parks on the grass because all the other parking spots are full. It's only five-thirty.

"I want you to ignore the media, no matter how distracting they are. Focus on what you want to say. Okay?" he says as he turns off the car.

"I can't believe they can come in and film whenever they want. I mean, I'm a minor." I unbuckle my seat belt. "It just doesn't seem right."

"All school board meetings are open forums, and anyone can attend. Public school business is handled in public. Always."

"I don't want to talk in front of the news." It's going to be hard enough talking to the school board.

They just look at each other and open their car doors. I know what they're thinking. I should've thought about that before I made certain choices that they'd force me to apologize for.

We stop to inspect the newly papered lobby, along

with the rest of Dogwood. Everyone young and old stops to peer at the walls. I blink up at the pages, not quite believing my eyes. *Coraline. The Outsiders.* And so many more. It's awesome. Mom frowns at a random page and ushers us to the auditorium, muttering under her breath.

We're forced to walk through the background behind a reporter broadcasting live from the auditorium doors. I pass by the lens quickly. If Kate saw me, she's probably yelling at the TV.

This time we don't sit in the front row because the media have their equipment stationed there. We sit center left. We're only ten feet from the podium; there's already a large camera sitting on a tripod in front of it.

The room has the same energy as at a sold-out show. People arrive early for good seats, and electricity crackles in the air. The school board is a bunch of men and one woman. It's weird not seeing Dad onstage with them, but he's with the PTSA, which is totally different from the school board. The PTSA is like a club that sells cookies and brings everyone together to try to make school a better place. The school board, though, can actually do things. They're the boss of everyone—the teachers, the principal, even the superintendent! Mom said most of the people on the board were really involved in their kids' schools years ago, and that's why they're there. I asked if they actually knew anything about education. Mom just looked at me funny.

The temperature rises as the seats fill up. Or maybe it's just me. I don't know. My throat is dry, and even though my hands feel like ice, my palms are dripping wet. I roll my dead-fish hands across my skinny jeans, but they're still just as clammy as ever.

I'm wearing tall brown boots with low heels and a long red sweater topped off with the pendant necklace Kate gave me.

The red matches the writing on my locker.

I push the cuticles back on my nails. I don't need to see who's here and who's not. Mom and Dad are going to make me speak no matter who shows up.

The lights flicker, but to my surprise, they stay on.

First, everyone stands for the Pledge of Allegiance. Once the audience settles back into their seats, the chairperson clears his throat. "Welcome, welcome. As a result of the alarming events of the last couple of days, we have called this emergency meeting. There are a few items on the agenda to discuss tonight. First, we need to resolve a teacher suspension. Second, we have a special request from a student who wishes to speak. Third, we will open the floor to community members. Remember, there is a five-minute time limit for each speaker."

He clears his throat again. "Item one. Natalie Bradshaw. She has been suspended due to her endorsement of unsuitable books for children. Tonight we will determine whether she will continue her employment here. Now, is Ms. Bradshaw present?"

I sit up straighter in my seat.

"I'm here," she says, standing near the front and approaching the podium. "I would like to address the board." She's wearing skinny jeans, dressy boots, and a blazer. Underneath it, her T-shirt reads BOOKS MATTER.

Definitely not the safe choice. She's my hero.

He sighs. "You have five minutes."

She places her hands on both sides of the podium and grips the edges.

The light on the camera facing the podium blinks red.

"When I was hired to be the librarian at Dogwood Middle, one of the requirements was that I provide access to books. I did exactly that."

There are a few snickers.

"Did I use poor judgment? I don't think so. You have so many bright young people who love books. And I've got news for you: letting your kids read about magic, about rebels, about subjects that may be controversial, won't lead them down the rabbit hole to failure. It will grow their humanity.

"That's why I do what I do. I believe children should have the opportunity to find themselves in books—scary ones, stories with adventure, characters who show them who they can be. They can handle it. They should also have the opportunity to meet different people in books. Yes, even people different from you. Is that not what education is? Broadening your knowledge from the world around you? Somewhere along the way, that has been forgotten.

"I'm sorry if some members of the community took offense at my actions. However, I stand by my choices. I would do it again in a heartbeat."

My mother gasps.

Ms. Bradshaw stands in silence and awaits her fate.

The chairperson taps the microphone and clears his throat once more to stop the murmurs running through the audience. "On the matter of continuing Natalie Bradshaw's employment by the town of Dogwood, how do you vote?"

"Nay."

"Nay."

I feel like I'm watching a train wreck in slow motion.

"Nay."

"Nay."

"Nay."

Dad reaches for Mom's hand. I can't believe this is happening.

"Nay."

"Nay."

It's over. There's a majority vote.

"Nay."

"Nay."

Ms. Bradshaw tenses, waiting for the final blow.

"Nay."

Many parents in the audience begin clapping, but surprisingly there are just as many boos. "Order, order," says the chairperson. "Let the record show that Natalie Bradshaw's employment by Dogwood Schools is terminated immediately."

Ms. Bradshaw turns around amid the camera flashes and strides up the aisle. Her mouth is set in a straight line, her shoulders squared. She looks fierce. I lean over my armrest, and her eyes meet mine. She squeezes my arm, just for a second, and says one word over the deafening applause.

"Groupie." And then she's gone.

I could cry. She was the best thing about Dogwood Middle. No question about it. She gave me somewhere I could just be me—not someone's crush, not a band geek, not the perfect kid. I could just *be*. And that made it the best place of all. My heart feels like it's frozen in place, and everything in me wants to howl at the unfairness of it.

Someone a few aisles up blows a foghorn in celebration and brings me back to Earth. Ms. Bradshaw is paying the price for my parents' actions, and I can't do anything about it.

But I can tell them what I think.

The chairperson speaks into the mic. "Next we have Alma June Harper, whose parents have arranged for her to speak. Ms. Harper, are you present?"

My legs carry me toward the podium, but I don't know how. They're about as supportive as jelly. Adrenaline grips my heart, thundering through my chest and unleashing a tidal wave of panic that wracks my entire being. Already, the sweat trickles under my arms. I knew I shouldn't have worn a sweater. I'm going to have pit stains down to my elbows before I even start. I pluck a note card from my back pocket with the apology that my parents helped me write.

And then a folded scrap of paper is pushed into my left hand, and Matt winks at me from his seat as I walk by. I take a deep breath and unfold it at the podium. It reads:

Who knew superheroes were Real? ☺ You've got this, Supergirl.

My shoulders relax just a touch, and I set Matt's message next to my speech.

"You have five minutes," the chairperson says.

I nod. This is it. No going back now. "Last month, I committed Dogwood's biggest crime. I checked out a book that some people thought was too scary for me."

The audience murmurs.

"There was nothing wrong with that book. And I *like* creepy. But no one listened. No one cared. Instead, they started a witch-hunt and drove out someone who helped me love books even more than I already did.

"So tonight, since we're all here over a book, I'm going to tell you a story." I crumple up my speech.

If Dad's eyes could throw daggers, I'd be covered in wounds. But it's my turn to speak, and I have four minutes and thirty-four seconds left.

"The author's visit was canceled. Yes, that's right. She

was going to travel here from across the country just to see us, and now she probably thinks we're ridiculous."

A man chuckles somewhere in a row close to me.

"Then they dumped the books they didn't like from the library. Our teachers had to fill out a form for every single thing we read that wasn't a textbook. But the school didn't stop there. They said we'd be punished if we had *unapproved texts*. In other words, no books allowed without permission.

"What good is an education that doesn't require us to think? You don't want us to read certain books because then we might ask the wrong questions. Instead, you'd rather give us test after test and then say our teachers have failed us.

"They have not.

"Ms. Bradshaw did not fail us.

"*You* are failing us.

"We need to think so we can figure things out for ourselves. Adults are always saying how we need to be responsible citizens, but how can we even learn what that means if you put the library on lockdown?

"I thought about all that. And when I found a book I wanted to read, I read it. Then other people asked to read it, so I said yes."

My eyes land on Abby in the crowd, and she gives me a knowing smile.

"It got bigger. Before I knew it, I had dozens of books and an empty locker to put them in. And you know what? Everyone started reading. I've never seen more students read at school in my life. It's now the coolest thing to do, all because you said we couldn't. It doesn't matter that you took our books away. We found more. Go ahead and rip down the writing on the walls if you want. But you can't change that we read them. It's in here now," I say with my hand over my heart. "And no matter what happens, you can't take that away from me. Or anyone else."

From the waist up, I'm perfectly still. From the podium down, I'm quite literally shaking in my boots.

"You forgot something in the middle of all this. We may be kids, but we're smarter than you think. We will always find a way to get around what you say if we don't agree with it. If you push, we will push back. If it's not me, it will be three more kids just like me. It's not going to go away. That's the reality. You can let us make reasonable choices about what we read, or you can wrap us in Bubble Wrap and watch us find a way around it.

"So what are you going to do? Are you going to keep punishing the whole school because we thought outside the box you tried to put us in? Will you do it in front of the entire nation?" I wave my arm toward the cameras. "They're watching.

"I'm *not* some troubled kid trying to destroy the community.

"I am outraged.

"I am censorship gone wrong."

I take a deep breath, brace my shoulders, and look directly into the camera lens. "I am the Rebel Librarian."

VERDICT

A collective gush of breath escapes the auditorium like air from a balloon. Lights pop in short bursts all around me, blinding and white and leaving dark splotches of brilliance when they go out. It overwhelms my senses. I focus on the video lens. It's the one camera without a flash in this whole place.

There are a few claps here and there, and then they morph into a slow clap. The beat grows faster and faster, rising over just as many boos. There's never been anything so divisive here. At least not while I've been alive.

The chairperson's voice rings out over the sound system. "Quiet, please! Quiet!"

He combs his fingers through a few wisps of white

hair, his fair skin turning a rosy red. "Young lady, I don't care if you *are* on national television. When you address the board, you should do it with respect!" He nods to the rest of the board.

I don't dare look at my parents. I can guess what they think about what I said. But I'm not ready to face that. I'm focused on this moment. On getting my chance to speak.

"Wait just a minute, Ms. Harper," a younger board member says. "You said a few things that I would like to address. Standardized tests are mandated by the state. We have no choice about that. I'm sorry if that clouds your idea of an ideal education, but it is what it is. And as for the books, we had every right to take them because they were found on school property. You lost all claim to them the moment you brought them on campus." He nods at the chairperson.

"You may be seated, Ms. Harper," the chairperson says.

I turn around to more popping lights. Every eye— human and electronic—in the entire place is on me. I slip into the aisle seat next to Mom and Dad. I can't help it. I'm completely shell-shocked.

"Item number three. Community members who wish to speak. Is there anyone who wishes to say a few words?"

Abby stands in the front. Matt raises his hand and

stands a few rows away. Dan pops up on the right. Then Olivia, who's still waiting for me to find one of the Warriors books. Colby. Brooke. Ryan, who told me how much he loved *The Crossover.* One by one, they rise until I can't see the school board members on the stage. Even Ms. Gibson stands, which blows my mind. I thought she taught *The Crucible* for a reason, but I wasn't expecting this. Then I notice the other English teachers also rising to their feet. There are probably eighty students standing, but I can't be sure—I can't see above the mass of people. So I stand with them.

Dad reaches out and tugs at my arm. I yank my arm away and remain standing.

The cameras bathe us in more light.

The chairperson's voice echoes off the walls. "What is this?"

More students stand.

"I don't know what kind of stunt you think you're pulling, but you cannot all speak."

I think we're speaking anyway.

"Sit down!"

"No!" comes a cry from near the front. "Listen to us!"

The cameras keep clicking.

"We have taken care of all official business. I see no

one over eighteen standing who is actually a contributing member of the community, so I move to adjourn. All in favor?" I guess teachers don't count, either.

Wadded-up pieces of paper whiz through the air toward the stage. This is going to turn ugly fast. Everyone standing hollers in protest.

The votes run through the table, all "ayes."

Someone darts to the podium, but I can't see over the guys standing a few rows ahead. "My name is Matt Brownlee, and I came here to speak tonight because your policy says I can. What you're doing is wrong, and you know it."

Pride swells deep in my chest. I peek at my mother out of the corner of my eye. She's frowning and shaking her head.

Matt says, "But it's not too late. You can still do the right thing and fix this. Whatever you do—"

"Point of order!" the chairperson yells, his complexion deepening to scarlet. He motions to someone off-stage. "Cut the mic!"

"Whatever you do, we're just going to find a way—"

The mic goes dead, and the telltale screech pings on my eardrums.

"Meeting adjourned. Thank you, and good night."

"You can't do that!" someone yells.

But the board has already disappeared behind the stage curtain.

"Let's go," Dad says. "This is getting out of hand." He and Mom nudge me along and out the double doors into the lobby.

The door shuts behind us, muffling the crowd's protests.

Reporters swarm like locusts the moment we emerge. "June! Tell us how you're feeling now. Do you agree with the verdict of the board?"

"Thank you, we'll be going now," Dad says, pushing his way through the crowd. "Excuse us."

I take a step to follow him and then stop. I think about Kate. There are cameras everywhere, and all I have to do is speak. "Wait." The reporters turn back to me. "I have something to say."

"June!"

"Sorry, Dad." I turn to the cameras. "I'm devastated. Ms. Bradshaw wanted us to think, so she didn't censor what we read. And it cost her her job. There's so much wrong with that, I just—I have no words."

A woman with ABC on her mic says, "June, talk to us about why you chose *Rebel Librarian* to describe yourself. Is it because you don't believe in rules?"

I blink a few times. "No, that's not it at all. I believe in the freedom to read. Most people around here would call that rebellion, so I thought I'd beat them to the punch."

"So if you could say one thing to America, what would it be?"

I glance over at my parents, who wear expressions of quiet horror. Then I take a deep breath. "Don't tell me what to read."

The reporter pivots and speaks into the lens. "Don't tell her what to read, folks. Live from Dogwood Middle, that was June Harper, the Rebel Librarian."

★

I sit at my favorite spot at the top of the stairs. Downstairs, Mom's and Dad's voices are clear.

Dad says, "Well, that was a disaster."

"It was. And the whole country saw it."

"Oh well. There's nothing we can do about it now."

"I thought about taking her out of school."

"NO!" He laughs. "Then she'd be here with us all day."

"I wish we could protect her forever."

Dad says, "We can sure try." He sighs. "I'm just so disappointed in her."

I drop my face into my hands and fight back the tears.

It's the first time I've ever heard my parents say they're disappointed in me.

Mom says, "The way she carried on like that in front of the whole world, and after we tried to guide her on what to say."

"I know," Dad agrees.

"Kate was so easy," Mom says. "She never did *anything* like this. I didn't see it coming." My sleeve is wet from wiping my face, but I can't pull myself away. I can't be Kate. I never was.

"You know what I think?"

"Hmm?" Mom says.

"I think June gets it from you." I look up midsniffle. My mom? A rule breaker?

"No, I think it's *you!*"

Dad laughs. "I'll tell her a story or two when she's older."

"Oh no you won't!"

They both laugh.

"She did a good job at the podium," Mom says. "Even if it wasn't what we wanted her to say."

I rest my chin on my hand. I wish I could've said what they wanted. I just couldn't.

"She did. Our kid is something else," Dad says.

"Which is why we have to ground her. Again."

"Absolutely. Can't wait to see what she does in high school."

"Bite your tongue." Mom sighs. "I'm just worried about—do you think June will ever look at us the way she used to?"

"Having regrets, are you?"

"No. We did the *right thing*. You know we did." Mom pauses. "Do you think she'll ever forgive us?" I lean my head against the wall and sigh. It's going to take some time, but I'll love them no matter what. They're my parents.

"Someday she will."

"But not today," she says.

Dad laughs. "Not a chance."

★

The shrill ring of the kitchen phone the next afternoon hurts my ears. I ignore it, just as I've been directed to ignore it all day long. Dad's checking the caller ID for the foreseeable future.

A sticky note on the counter says *Call your sister.* I pitch it into the trash and do a double take. Under a pile of coffee grounds and orange peel, I can make out the word READ printed on newspaper. I glance toward Dad's office and back toward the stairwell. I fish what's left of the *Dogwood Gazette* out of the trash.

DON'T TELL ME WHAT TO READ is the headline. Below it, there's a picture of me standing at the podium. Another picture shows most of the students in the auditorium refusing to sit. There are even more students than I thought. And finally, there's a picture of Ms. Bradshaw's face when she hears the final vote. She looks heartbroken but not defeated. Resolved but not angry.

I take a trembling breath and will myself to read the words.

> *Educational leaders were thrown a curveball last night when local students fought back against censorship at the Dogwood school board meeting. Seventh grader June Harper said, "You can let us make reasonable choices about what we read, or you can wrap us in Bubble Wrap and watch us find a way around it."*
>
> *School board members have not returned—*

Footsteps thud from the next room. I quickly stuff the paper back in the trash and swipe a bran muffin from the stove. The phone rings again.

"Do you realize that every single search engine is

going to have your name in it now because of this?" Mom sips coffee in the living room with her back to the kitchen. "Not because of music awards or being accepted to an Ivy League school. Because of this." But not every adult is like my parents. Ms. Bradshaw taught me that. Some people might even like what I did.

"I know." The phone rings half a ring, then stops.

"This is who you're always going to be now." Sadness laces Mom's voice.

"This is who I am." I'm not Kate, and Kate isn't even who they wanted her to be. I'm me. It's about time I figured it out.

Mom brings the mug to her lips and blows across the surface. "I hope you don't regret it, honey."

"No. It's worth it."

She tilts her face over her shoulder and reveals dark, puffy rings under her eyes. "Does Ms. Bradshaw think it's worth it?"

My pulse quickens. Try to stay calm. Try to stay calm.

The phone rings again.

"That's not fair."

"Oh, it's plenty fair. How was it you put it last night? 'If it's not me, it will be three more kids just like me. It's not going to go away.'" She shrugs a shoulder. "Same rule applies to the parents. If it's not us, it'll be three more just like us."

I'd hoped somehow that I'd get through to her, but she still doesn't get it. I have to make her understand. "Maybe you're right, Mom. But those three other parents didn't do it. You did. And now you have to live with it."

She faces away again.

Could it be she's actually sorry about Ms. Bradshaw? I have to know. "Was it worth it?" I ask.

She crosses her legs and settles into the couch. "I wouldn't change a thing."

My shoulders fall. I think about how hard it was to figure out how to be myself when it wasn't allowed. How the thought of breaking my parents' hearts kept me awake at night. I couldn't stop asking myself if it was the right thing to do. And then one day, I knew the answer. I sigh. "It's okay, Mom. Neither would I."

I run upstairs with the phone and dial Kate's number.

She answers on the first ring. "June?"

"It's me."

"Oh my gosh! They just played your speech on the *Today* show."

"Seriously? The *Today* show?" I saw all the cameras there, but I never dreamed it would get this big.

"You're on *every show*. It's like the whole country picked up the story."

"You're kidding!" They put a password on the remote control after my performance last night, so I can't check.

"No, and now it's turned into some kind of national debate. You've got everyone talking. The ladies on *The View*, and *Ellen*—oh my gosh, *Ellen*! She opened her show dancing up and down the aisles and giving banned books to audience members. She called the dance the Junebug and dedicated it to you!"

"She what?" My brain can't keep up with this. It's all happening so fast. Ellen DeGeneres? It's more than I could've hoped for in a million years. "I had no idea. Dad's screening all the calls, and I've been under lock and key. Feel free to call with info from the outside."

"I will. How are Mom and Dad doing with all this?"

I shrug. "Mom is pretty upset. Dad won't even look at me."

She laughs. "That's because you won this round."

If this is winning, I'd hate to see what losing looks like. "I didn't win. I'm still grounded, we lost Ms. Bradshaw, and everything is still the same."

"Trust me," Kate says, a hint of a wry smile in her voice. "You won."

FORGOTTEN EMBERS

Everything is gray and cold just before dusk. The trees, the dying grass, the sky. Emma sits at the end of my driveway just like she used to on school mornings.

"Hi," she says.

"Hey."

"I've been calling all day, but I couldn't get through." Her eyes are puffy and red. There's no makeup on her face. She looks a lot like my best friend, before the last month made her a different person.

I say nothing.

"Are you okay?" she asks.

I sit down next to her. "Why are you here, Emma?"

She presses her lips together and looks up at the old

oak tree we used to play under. "I was wrong. Okay? I screwed up, and I can't take it back." She wipes her face on her coat sleeve and looks at me. "I wish I could, June. I'd take it all back."

"He dumped you, didn't he?"

She sobs. "Yes." She shakes her head. "But I'm more upset about losing my best friend."

I hug my knees. "Me too."

"All I wanted the last two days was to call and tell you how sorry I am." She looks me right in the eye. "And I am. Sorry."

"I know."

We sit in silence under the deepening gray sky, our breath creating a fog around us.

"Do you think it will ever be the same between us?" Emma asks.

I turn to her. "I don't think it can be."

Her lower lip trembles. "I know. And I get it."

I reach out and squeeze her arm. "But maybe we can try."

She squeezes back. "I'd love that." She sighs. "For what it's worth, I'll always wish I'd been a part of all this."

I rest my chin in my hand and smile. "You kind of were."

She looks at me blankly. "What?"

"Remember how you gave me *The Graveyard Book*?"

"Yeah."

I shrug. "It was part of my library."

She shakes her head and grins. "Good. I'm glad."

We rise to our feet.

"So, I'll see you in band?" I ask.

"Yeah," she says with a wistful smile. "I'll see you."

When she heads home, I dart a look back at the house. I'm grounded, but right now there's somewhere I need to go.

I shiver in my down coat and walk toward Maple Lane. The first thing I notice is the U-Haul in the driveway of the house with the Little Free Library. The front door is cracked open, even though it's freezing outside.

For the first time ever, I bypass the Little Free Library and hike up the driveway. I can't help but peek inside the fogged windowpane. Boxes stand in neat rows, with a roll of packing tape and markers stacked on top.

"Hello?" I call.

There's no answer. I've seen enough movies to know better than to walk into someone's house uninvited, so I ring the doorbell.

"Just a minute!" a deep voice yells.

I can't believe I'm just ringing the doorbell, but I have to. If I do nothing else today, I need to meet them.

Someone in jeans, boots, and a flannel shirt walks around the corner with a stack of boxes labeled FRAGILE hiding his face. He drops them to the floor with a clatter. "Can I help you?" His dark eyes blaze under his short black hair, and the faintest bit of stubble traces his jaw.

"Hi, um. I wanted to ask about your library."

"Oh, that's not mine. Hang on." He walks around the corner and hollers, "Honey! I need you a minute!"

Footsteps creak on the old wooden floors.

And there's Ms. Bradshaw in jeans and a ponytail, looking years younger than I remember her. Her T-shirt reads I LIKE BIG BOOKS (AND I CANNOT LIE). She's glowing.

I struggle to make my mouth work. "It was you? The whole time?"

She grins. "You found me."

"I wanted it to be you!" My eyes fill with tears, and I quickly wipe them away.

The incredibly good-looking guy glances from her to me and clears his throat.

"Oh, sorry," she says. "June, this is Brendan. Brendan, June."

"Brendan," I say, my voice traveling up an octave.

"Nice to meet you. Although I have to say I already knew who you were. From the news." Brendan winks.

Of course he did. Who didn't see June Harper twirling in the national spotlight?

"Hon, June and I are going to catch up. Would you finish packing the books?"

"I'm on it," he says, ducking to kiss her on the cheek. "Nice meeting you, June."

"You too."

"Come on in," she says. "How about some hot chocolate?"

"I'd love some." I could say something else, like *I'm sorry; please forgive me* or *It wasn't your fault; it was mine.* Instead, I trail after her to the kitchen and try to find the words I need to say.

She produces two mugs, fills them with water, and starts the microwave. I take the seat next to her at the table.

"You're moving." I feel ridiculous the moment the words are out of my mouth. Of course she's moving. No one rents a U-Haul unless they're going somewhere with a lot of stuff. "I didn't think it would be so soon."

"They didn't give me a lot of choice," she said.

"I feel so bad about it. All of it." That does nothing to fill the hole in my bleeding conscience.

The microwave beeps.

"I know you do, and you shouldn't. I knew exactly what I was doing."

"You'd still have your job if it weren't for me."

"For a while, anyway. But there are things I wouldn't have." She stirs a cocoa packet into each mug and hands one to me. The heat warms my palms.

"I wouldn't have an amazing job waiting for me in Boston. And get this—they say I can fill my library with all the banned books I want." She blows on her mug.

I guess I look surprised, because she says, "June, millions of people saw us on the news this week. Especially you and your message after the meeting ended. My phone has been ringing off the hook with job offers! It's surreal. One TV show even asked me for an exclusive."

"I'm really happy for you," I say. "I just wish it hadn't happened that way."

"But it did, and it's done." She sips her hot chocolate.

I wish I could be like her and quit dwelling on my part in this. "Can I ask you something?"

"Shoot."

"Why did you give away all of Brendan's books?"

She puts down her mug. "Ah, groupie. You go straight for the heart, don't you?"

"I guess. Sorry, I just—I couldn't figure it out."

She tilts her head. "I suppose I can tell you now." She smiles. "I met Brendan in college, and we were so in love we couldn't see straight. I thought everything would line up neat and pretty after we graduated, but sometimes things don't work out that way. And sometimes—if you focus on the wrong things—you let a great love slip away."

"I knew it was a love story!" I can't wait to tell Matt I was right.

"So when I landed the job here, I told him it would be too hard to stay together long-distance. I just couldn't do that to him."

"Um, have you *seen* him? What were you thinking?"

She laughs. "Yeah, I know. Genius move. So when I finally figured out I'd made the biggest mistake of my life, I sent him a heartbook."

"A what?"

"A book that touched my heart—there are so many of those. And then I sent another. And another. For three months, I sent him a book every single day. And every single package came back unopened. 'Return to sender.'"

"Oh no!"

"It turns out he had moved. His old roommate didn't bother to tell him about the packages, either, because Brendan had been so upset when I left."

"That's awful!"

"I guess I deserved it, though. So the day I left Dogwood Middle, I came home and put together the Little Free Library. I'd ordered it over the summer and gotten so busy with school that I hadn't taken the time to put it together. I had all these books, and I hoped maybe they'd find someone who needed them. I waited each morning and afternoon, but no one really checked it out except for the little ones down the street. And then I was drinking coffee by the window one morning, and there you were."

"I saw you."

She laughs. "I know. I tried so hard to sneak. I couldn't let you know it was me."

"I wish you had."

"June, because you shared those books, my sending them to Brendan meant something, even though he never received them. And then it got so much better. The Dogwood reporter did a segment before the PTSA meeting about the mysterious books found in a locker, all addressed to 'Brendan.'"

I remember Mr. Beeler waving a book around and talking to the reporter.

She places her hand on my arm and beams at me. "He saw it. Of course, he didn't think much of it at the time. Just that I lived here and there were a bunch of books addressed to a Brendan. But then he saw the headlines from the national news, and there was no doubt in his mind. He got in the car and drove straight through the night. I found him on my doorstep yesterday morning with coffee and doughnuts."

"No way."

"I don't kid about books. Ever."

I laugh. "Yeah, you mentioned that." I trace the edge of the table with my thumb. "I'm glad it worked out for you. I just—I feel like everything was pointless. Look at what happened. Look at what you lost. Don't you worry it was all for nothing?"

"It wasn't for nothing, June. Nothing ever is."

"They're not going to change."

"Not today. But they will. I don't think anyone's ever told them they're wrong before, do you?" Her face is full of mischief.

My parents? I laugh. "Definitely not."

"That takes a while to settle in. It'll take even longer before they do something about it."

I sigh. "Meanwhile, you're escaping and I'm stuck here."

"Dogwood needs you, June."

I shake my head. "I wish I could believe that."

"Give it time. Change happens slowly, but what you have to remember is that it *happens*. Even when you can't see it. And then one day, there it is."

I think about my watercolor painting of the leaves.

"Someday you'll get to go away to college. Maybe you'll end up in Boston."

"Maybe." It's more than a maybe. It's the thought of walls upon walls of books, and Ms. Bradshaw handing me a stack of novels. I *see* it, and the little flame in my chest flares.

"I heard you were going out with the Whitmore kid. If you are, promise me you won't give up who you are to make him happy." Looking at my shocked face, she says, "I've been dying to say it, and I wasn't about to miss the chance to set you straight."

"I ended it. He wanted me to choose between books and him."

"And good riddance." She takes a sip from her mug.

I half grin. "There's someone else, actually."

"Do tell."

"He tried to speak at the meeting, but they cut him off—"

"Oh, the Brownlee kid! I saw that on the news."

"Yeah."

"Does he have a problem with you being awesome, or does he actually let you shine?"

"He helped me run the library."

"Hmm. He risked it all for books?" She grins. "Or for you?"

"He actually gave me a book from his own collection as a gift. Like you did with Brendan."

She raises an eyebrow. "And did it work?"

I blush.

She cackles. "Every time! Oh, he's good. Watch out for that one. He's making a play straight for your sentimental heart. Trust me."

I do trust her. So much.

If life were perfect, I'd be able to spend the evening in this cozy little kitchen, but I know I can't stay. "I should probably get going," I say. "You have tons of packing left to do." And I'm eternally grounded.

"Hang on a sec—I have something for you," she says. She disappears into another room. When she returns, she carries a manila envelope with *June* written on it. "I was going to put this in the Little Free Library, but now that you're here, I'll leave it with you."

"Thanks." I wish I had something for her, but it's not like this was planned.

Before I can rip into it, she says, "Open it later, okay?"

I nod. This is the moment I've been dreading since I saw her walk around the corner. I shake my head. "I don't want to say goodbye."

"Then we won't." She hugs me, and I squeeze back. I think she believes in me more than anyone else on the planet, and she's leaving me. I don't want to let her go. I need her to talk to me about books, to show me how to leave the past behind me. Most of all, I need her to teach me how to survive Dogwood without her in it.

"I'm so proud of you, June. If you ever think it was for nothing, it wasn't. You were reason enough for all of this. The rest of it was just gravy."

I laugh. Tears sting my eyes and brim at the edges. "Stop it. You're going to make me cry."

She pulls away and smiles. Her eyes glisten, and her face is splotchy. "My email is in the package. Keep in touch and let me know what you're reading, okay? I'll see you later, groupie."

I press my lips and try to hold it together. "See you later," I squeak. And then I force my legs to carry me out the door and down the driveway.

As soon as I'm out of sight of her house, I rip into the package. I flip it over in my hands and suck in my breath. *The Makings of a Witch.* I sit on the curb and flip to the inside page. There, in the same blue ink as all the inscriptions to Brendan, it reads:

> To June, who learned that one
> book can change everything . . .
> But none of it would've been possible
> if it hadn't been for her.
> —Ms. B.

The weight of her words covers me like quick-dry chocolate on a Dairy Queen cone. That she would want me to have this book . . . the one that started it all on that day that feels like ages ago. The corner is creased, and the Dogwood Middle library sticker remains. I snicker. Thief. This is a banned book if ever I've seen one. It's so light in my hands. Misleading, really. The words are much heavier than anyone would guess.

So much has changed that I wonder if it will feel

different when I read it again. If you're one person when you read a book, and then you change, does the book become different? Do the words stretch to fit the new version of who you are?

I smile. *The Velveteen Rabbit* did.

All I need is one book. That's all it takes.

And then I'll start another library.

By the time I make it home, the sky is dark blue against the sparks shooting up from the fire pit in the backyard. There's no ringing phone on the stone patio. Just the smell of firewood and the luminous stars, some shining more brightly than others. It's like they're winking at me with some secret the universe isn't ready to tell. Beneath them, the yard is dotted with piles of leaves.

Dad leans back in the Adirondack chair, staring at the crumbling logs, his favorite mug brimming with coffee.

"Hey, Dad." This silent treatment can't last forever. "Yard looks good."

He sips his coffee. "Your art teacher emailed me. Mr. Garcia. Someone from the high school visited and noticed your painting. Says you're invited to take high school art next year."

I can't help but smile. Someone actually liked it?

I don't know what to say. I guess it really was all about the layers. And change.

"June, I know you love art, but I want you to give some serious thought to your future."

It's time to tell him. "I already have."

He looks relieved. It's like the stress rolls off his shoulders in waves. "And?"

"It's dangerous, but I'll be saving lives." The stars are so bright, I could reach out and touch them. I think I might.

"Doctors Without Borders?" he asks.

"No. I'm going to be a librarian."

TITLES IN JUNE'S LIBRARY

The Crossover, Kwame Alexander

Six of Crows, Leigh Bardugo

Doll Bones, Holly Black

Blubber, Judy Blume

Poppy Mayberry, The Monday, Jennie K. Brown

Sticks & Stones, Abby Cooper

Matilda, Roald Dahl

The Witches, Roald Dahl

Because of Winn-Dixie, Kate DiCamillo

Better Nate Than Ever, Tim Federle

Coraline, Neil Gaiman

The Graveyard Book, Neil Gaiman

George, Alex Gino

Escape from Mr. Lemoncello's Library, Chris Grabenstein

The Outsiders, S. E. Hinton

Diary of a Wimpy Kid, Jeff Kinney

EngiNerds, Jarrett Lerner

A Snicker of Magic, Natalie Lloyd

Rules, Cynthia Lord

Number the Stars, Lois Lowry

Bob, Wendy Mass and Rebecca Stead

Bridge to Terabithia, Katherine Paterson

Pax, Sara Pennypacker

The Lightning Thief, Rick Riordan

Harry Potter and the Sorcerer's Stone, J. K. Rowling

Dork Diaries 1: Tales from a Not-So-Fabulous Life,
    Rachel Renée Russell

Holes, Louis Sachar

The Secret Horses of Briar Hill, Megan Shepherd

Goosebumps series, R. L. Stine

Roll of Thunder, Hear My Cry, Mildred D. Taylor

Wolf Hollow, Lauren Wolk

Brown Girl Dreaming, Jacqueline Woodson

OTHER TITLES IN THIS BOOK

The Makings of a Witch*

Wishtree, Katherine Applegate

Tales of a Fourth Grade Nothing, Judy Blume

Beezus and Ramona, Beverly Cleary

Lily and Dunkin, Donna Gephart

Old Yeller, Fred Gipson

Twilight, Stephenie Meyer

The Crucible, Arthur Miller

Anne of Green Gables, L. M. Montgomery

Monster, Walter Dean Myers

Junie B. Jones series, Barbara Park

The Little Prince, Antoine de Saint-Exupéry

The Hobbit, J. R. R. Tolkien

The Velveteen Rabbit, Margery Williams

---

* Fictional title

ACKNOWLEDGMENTS

Thank you to my editor, Caroline Abbey, for partnering with me to make this book better in every imaginable way. You get me, and I love working with you. To Michelle Nagler and Mallory Loehr, my publishers, a huge thank-you for taking a chance on a rebel librarian and a debut author. To Mary McCue, Emily Bamford, Hannah Black, Emily Petrick, and everyone on the publicity and marketing team, I am so grateful for everything you've done to promote this book. To Leslie Mechanic, cover designer, and Andy Smith, cover artist, your work is so beautiful that it made me cry when I saw it for the first time. Thank you so much for capturing the essence of June Harper. And to the entire team at Random House Children's Books, thank you for working tirelessly on this book.

To my agent and friend, Rick Richter, I am so lucky to have you on this journey with me. You believed in this book from the very beginning. Thank you for everything.

Sarah Malley, you are my publishing fairy godmother. You plucked me out of the slush—twice—and changed my life with an email. None of this would have happened without you. Thank you from the bottom of my heart.

This book is a love letter to all the educators and librarians who put books in my hands and nurtured my love of stories. Some in particular also thought I should be holding a pen, and they can't begin to know what it has meant to me. To Dr. Susan Groenke, thank you for listening to my idea for this novel and telling me that I *had* to write it. To Dr. Bill Larsen, you once told me that if I finished one project, I'd finish everything. You were right. And a most heartfelt thank-you to Dr. Jo Angela Edwins, who sent me a Christmas card every year for fifteen years, each with a note to "Keep writing." Those words of encouragement added up and meant quite a lot. Thank you all for the gentle nudges and kicks over the years.

A huge thank-you to Natasha Neagle and Kesi Thomas for reading my first draft and offering valuable critiques and feedback. I am so grateful to both of you for your love, support, and friendship. Many thanks to Amber Rountree for answering my school board questions. And to Tricia Holman Gillentine, Dr. Stacey Reece, Dr. Rachelle Savitz, Dr. Elizabeth MacTavish, Dr. Geri Landry, Jessica Mangicaro, Danielle Selah, Crystal Braeuner, Joanna

O'Hagan, Katie Bailey, and Olivia Hinebaugh, thank you for so many encouraging words over the years. I heard them all.

To Matt and Leigh Ann Jernigan, thank you for the pep talks, support, and guacamole when I needed it most.

Finally, an enormous thank-you to my sweet family, who survived seasons of my daydreaming while I wrote and revised this novel. And most especially, thank you to my mom, who read it first.

ABOUT THE AUTHOR

Like librarian Ms. Bradshaw in *Property of the Rebel Librarian*, Allison Varnes has fought for her students. She taught English in special education for eight years, and once had to convince administrators that *The Lion, the Witch and the Wardrobe* and the Harry Potter books were not endorsements of witchcraft. She has a PhD in education from the University of Tennessee. And like her book's heroine, June, Allison is a former marching-band geek. When she's not writing, she howls along to the *Hamilton* soundtrack with a quartet of Chihuahuas named after the Peanuts gang.

Find her on Twitter at @allisonvarnes or on Facebook at facebook.com/allisonvarnesauthor.